T0062436

The Vision Quest

Colin Broadbent

Order this book online at www.trafford.com
or email orders@trafford.com

Most Trafford titles are also available at major online book retailers.

Printed in Victoria, BC, Canada.

ISBN: 978-1-4269-2188-9 (soft)
ISBN: 978-1-4269-2189-6 (hard)

Library of Congress Control Number: 2009913884

*Our mission is to efficiently provide the world's finest, most comprehensive
book publishing service, enabling every author to experience success.
To find out how to publish your book, your way, and have it
available worldwide, visit us online at www.trafford.com*

Trafford rev. 12/23/2009

Trafford
PUBLISHING® www.trafford.com

North America & international
toll-free: 1 888 232 4444 (USA & Canada)
phone: 250 383 6864 ♦ fax: 812 355 4082

Chapter 1   The Wagon Train.

ACROSS THE NORTH American prairie in the year 1875 a wagon train wound its way slowly and cautiously. Eleven wagons in all, hoping, nay, expecting to reach the promised land of the West coast of the U.S.A.; Oregon or thereabouts. The train was making its way across an open plain with a distant view of the Dakota Black Hills to the North and a high bluff to the South. In front the way was clear, only grass and scrub and the odd tree. As it made its way ever Westward towards the Shangri-La of Oregon its progress was watched by a keen pair of eyes which noted every little detail of its composition.

A lone rider, a white man, sat his horse on the summit of the high bluff to the South. The wagon train was passing almost beneath his feet. The bluff was an extensive one stretching a mile or more in an East-West direction. At the Eastern end it gradually tapered down to meet the prairie, at the Western end it ended abruptly in a sudden and dangerous precipice.

The man and his horse looked down on the wagons from a height of some eighty or ninety feet; eighty or ninety feet of sheer drop. The wall of the bluff was almost vertical; a few channels cut its face in a downwards direction. Normally they would be water-filled but now, in the summer they were dry; there had been no rain for some considerable time. A few stunted trees, similarly deprived of water dotted side of the bluff. Near the bottom scattered cacti were to be found. A myriad of loose rocks and a few more firmly fixed boulders here and there completed the picture.

Nevertheless, the rider intended to descend the bluffs at that particular spot; he had business with the wagon-train.

The name of this intrepid rider was Charles Cunningham. Ex captain in the U.S.army. How he came to be there was a long story. About twenty-five years of age he had a glittering career before him, or so it had seemed. Now he was an ex officer from the army. There were several theories as to how this had come about.

He had been disgusted by the government's and army's treatment of the Indians, and had gone off to live with them and to better understand them and their way of life.

Another theory was that he had been court-martialled for insubordination and, to avoid the inevitable reduction in rank, had taken refuge with the Sioux.

Yet another theory held that he had not been court-martialled only threatened with it; to avoid the possibility he had joined with the Sioux.

Finally there was the tale that he had resigned his commission and gone to the Indians to escape the attentions of a girl who had designs on him. He had tried to get a posting far away without success, the girl had followed him to the fort and elsewhere in a vain endeavour to get his attention.

Anyway, whatever the reason he had been living with the Ogallala Sioux now almost a year. In that time the Sioux had attacked and overwhelmed three wagon trains and were about to serve this one in the same way.

Charles Cunningham had pleaded with the chiefs and elders of the tribe to allow him to talk with the leader of the wagon train in an attempt to get them to change their route which took them through the Sioux hunting grounds and perilously close to their sacred burial ground.

They had been scornful about his idea; the "White eyes" would not listen. What did they care about the Sioux? Nevertheless Charles had persisted with his plea. In the end they had relented a little. He could warn the wagon train about the danger of pursuing their journey and get them to change direction. The Sioux would wait in ambush somewhere further along the trail in the expectation of his failure.

Charles knew that they wouldn't give him long to change the wagonners minds; about half-an-hour at the most. They were very angry about the constant invasions of their lands; they would show no mercy.

Charles Cunningham was a tall man, about six foot or as near as made little difference; he had fair hair, blue eyes and eyebrows which matched his hair. Apart from side whiskers he was clean-shaven. Those whiskers were quite long, reaching down to his lower jaw. He kept them well trimmed however. He was strongly built with broad shoulders and slim hips.

Charles wore dark blue trousers tucked into his riding boots and a blue and red checked shirt. Around his waist was a gun-belt and holster holding an Army 0.45 Colt six-gun. He also sported a cartridge belt with a Bowie knife attached at his left hip. A stetson, cream-coloured adorned his head. His horse was an Indian pony, very wiry and strong. The usual saddle and saddle- bags completed his outfit apart from the Winchester rifle which was carried in a scabbard near his left leg.

The wagon-train approached slowly, it was about level with him now; he knew he would have to move swiftly if he wanted to keep them from the Sioux.

The nearest and most dangerous way was straight down the almost vertical side of the bluffs. He would have to do it though if he wanted to warn the wagon-train before it was too late.

He urged his pony over the edge of the bluffs; the animal was reluctant but his rider persevered. With his ears pricked up and snorting his displeasure, the pony commenced his descent. He braced his fore-legs hard against the slope while his hind-legs were flexed as hard as could be; his hind quarters were almost touching the ground. In this rather undignified posture animal and man descended. An occasional push with his hind-legs kept up the downward motion, not that there was much need for that for the steepness of the bluff was almost enough to keep horse and rider moving swiftly downwards. The intelligent Indian pony avoided the dangerous network of dried-up water channels which ran down the face of the bluff, likewise the sparsely scattered trees. His rider was experienced and skilful enough to allow him to find his own way down; he sat almost motionless on the pony's back. He maintained an almost upright posture during the descent leaning slightly backwards.

At last the lower slopes were reached, the pony, snorting his relief, assumed a more dignified stance and proceeded to wind his way through the maze of cacti which now prevailed.

Reaching the floor of the prairie at last, Charles Cunningham glanced up at the wagon-train. He and his pony had raised a large dust cloud during their descent; there was no sign from the wagon-train.

"Pretty poor look-out they must keep," he thought.

He urged his pony to a canter and approached the leading wagon.

The man on the front seat glanced at him but otherwise took little heed.

Charles signalled to him to stop.

Somewhat reluctantly the fellow obeyed. He looked sourly at Charles.

"What can I do fer you, mister?" He asked.

"You heading for Oregon?" Charles asked.

"What if we are? What's it to yuh?"

Charles explained,

"You're heading into trouble mister. This here's Sioux hunting ground. They don't take kindly to people intruding. Scares away the buffalo. If yuh care to let me guide yuh for a spell I can show you another way to the West coast."

The man spat over the side of the wagon.

"Yuh crazy or what? We aim to get to Oregon come what may. We don't give a cuss about the Sioux or anyone else. Yuh're wasting yuh time mister. So long!"

The sour faced middle aged female sitting next to him on the wagon nodded her agreement.

"That's so Silas. Don't need nobody to tell us what to do. We spoke to an army patrol a while back. The lieutenant told us there weren't any Indians around here."

"Well, ma,am, he was wrong,"Charles replied, "there's plenty of Indians about here if you know how to look. They're fixing to attack you pretty soon."

Silas spat again.

"Count the wagons mister. Eleven ain't they? That means around twenty or so rifles. We can take care of a whole tribe of Sioux or whatever they call themselves. Anyway, how come yuh know so much about their plans? Seems to me you are mighty well informed."

Charles didn't answer him. What was the use?

"Suit yourself mister," he said, "mind if I try some of the other wagons?"

The other shook his reins and got his wagon rolling once more.

"If yuh want to try mister that's up to you. So long."

Charles tried the other wagons one by one as each rolled on by him. It was useless; they took no notice of his warnings, one or two even jeered at him. At length he came to the last wagon of all. It was straggling a little way behind the rest of the train. As it came up to him he saw that it was being driven by a rather attractive lady of round about thirty years of age. She was handling the horses pretty well. The blue dress she was wearing fitted her figure perfectly and was drawn up to just above her knees.

Her legs thus exposed were very nice and shapely, her knees also. She was slightly tanned by the sun in a most attractive way.

She halted the wagon as she came up to Charles. She smiled on him.

"What can I do for you mister?" She asked.

Charles began his warnings about the Sioux; he wasn't going to get anywhere he felt sure. Nor was he mistaken. She shook her head;

"Sorry mister, we follow the others. They'll take care of us."

"Who is 'us'?" asked Charles.

"Why us here in this wagon. My friends and myself. There's Freda and Josephine."

Just then a woman's head appeared from behind the girl.

"What's the matter Sarah?" She asked.

Sarah answered,

"Fellow here claims we are trespassing on Sioux hunting grounds. He wants us to follow him as he takes us by a different route to Oregon."

Charles touched his hat politely to the other female.

"That's right miss. The Sioux are fixing to attack you pretty soon."

Freda shook her head.

"We don't fall fer that one, mister. How do we know we can trust you? Get us out on the trail alone with you and who knows what you'll do. Besides which we don't mean no harm to the Sioux. If it comes to a fight we got enough men here to stand them off."

Charles was growing impatient.

"That all you got in this wagon? Just the three of you? You're in fer a nasty surprise when the Sioux do attack. Won't you listen to me? Look' I'll hand over my gun and

Bowie knife to you if you'll just listen to me and let me lead you all to safety."

The two females shook their heads, Josephine was apparently asleep in the back of the wagon, they were going to stick with the rest of the train. There was safety in numbers.

Charles gave up then. He turned his horse away and rode off towards the bluffs once more. He made no attempt to scale the heights but, instead, he headed towards the Eastern end where it came down to the prairie. There he made his way across the plain for several miles until he came to the village of the Ogallala Sioux.

He rode over to the pony herd where the remainder of the ponies were kept. Most of them were out with the war party. He dismounted, removed his saddle, blankets and rifle, and turned his pony loose to be looked after by a young Indian boy of about ten years of age.

He went slowly to his tepee which, until a short time ago, he had shared with three young Sioux. In the last few months they had left one by one to get married; the last one only two weeks ago. In the tepee he laid down his rifle, saddle and blankets and then his gun-belt and six-gun, also his Bowie knife. He brushed the dust from his clothes, took a drink of water, tended to the fire, and went forth to visit his friend Bear-Paw.

Chapter 2   Bear-Paw.

THE DIVISIONS OF the Plains Indians were far more complex than simply those between the tribes. Each tribe was closely related to a number of others linguistically. There were also more distinct tribal divisions, and subsequent ramifications into sub-tribes, hunting bands and clans The Sioux nation was initially divided into three separate entities over a period of time. These were, the Dakotas, or Santee Sioux; the Nakotas,or Yankton Sioux; and the Lakotas. The first two tribes remained on the eastern edge of the plains, but the Lakotas or Teton Sioux migrated west to the central plains, and became known as the western Sioux.

Although the number fluctuated slightly as divisions disbanded or united, there were strictly seven sub-tribes of the Teton Sioux. This number was considered integral to the nation's structure.

These sub-tribes were; the Brule Sioux, The Hunkpapa Sioux, the Miniconjou Sioux, the Ogallala Sioux, the Oohenonpah Sioux, the Sans Arc and Sihasapa Sioux.

These sub-tribes still contained too many people to be practical units outside the summer months and so the Plains tribes divided into compact hunting bands. These were small enough to be mobile and to require only a limited amount of food and grazing, yet remained large enough to defend themselves and to co-operate as a unit when hunting the buffalo.

The lodge or tipi provided shelter for all the tribes of the Plains. It was basically a tilted cone, comprising three or four main poles strapped together at the top with sinew. It was covered with dressed buffalo skins. The lower quarter had a draught-excluding buffalo-hide liner on the inside and a narrow entrance facing east covered by a skin-flap.

The tipi was capable of being transported easily; the poles presented the greatest difficulty, but they could be easily be dragged by two or three horses and they could also carry the lodge cover. The tipi could be dismantled or erected quickly by two experienced women and the protection it offered was excellent. It was strong enough to endure the harshest winters, being water-proof and stream-lined against the wind. It could be easily patched if damaged. At the top were two smoke-flaps each positioned by an outer pole. These simple devices could be positioned according to the direction and strength of the wind, preventing draughts and allowing free exit of smoke from a central fire, and so ensuring warmth in the winter.

The tipi could be considered as more than just a shelter as it embodied the sacred circular form, and was seen to be symbolic of the Indian's world. The painting of visionary experiences and war exploits on the lodge cover, door and liner was common.

The Plains Indians were a very spiritual people believing that supernatural power pervaded every aspect of their life; to live in harmony with that power was essential to their survival. A manifestation of that spiritual power was called 'wakan' by the Sioux. A holy man was therefore called 'Wikasa- Wacan'. Their supreme deity was 'Wakan-Tanka' or the Great Spirit. 'Wakan' power was the source of what came to be known as medicine, so that 'making medicine' simply meant invoking the Sacred Powers. Medicine was sought and held through prayer, self induced visions, ritual and medicine items such as pipes and other bundles. It was so important because it provided for the tribe and guided warriors and healers.

A belief in the Supreme deity or Great Spirit was universal, the original source of 'medicine'. The sun was regarded as a material token of the Great Spirit's existence. While the Great Spirit was an abstract, the sun was a visible symbol, and the tipi was always pitched to face east so that prayers of thanks could be offered up to it at the beginning of each day.

Charles walked slowly towards the tipi of Bear-Paw his mind on the fate of the wagon-train. It would all be over by now, he thought. Soon the war-party would be returning with its booty and maybe a prisoner or two. He sighed; ah well he had tried to get them to turn back, they were stubborn and foolish like so many of their kind.

Outside the entrance to Bear-Paw's tipi he saw 'Sweet Prairie Blossom' the number one squaw of Bear-Paw squatting by a fire cooking the evening meal. She was a pleasant looking young woman of about twenty-nine years of age. 'Sweet Prairie Blossom' had borne two sons to Bear-Paw, the eldest being then eleven years old. She was, as always, pleased to see Charles. "Ho, Charlee, how are you? The day went well with you? Bear-Paw will be glad to see you. He awaits within. Please enter."

Charles greeted her in his usual friendly fashion and, pushing aside the tipi flap, he entered the tipi. Bear-Paw was seated on a buffalo robe smoking his pipe; his face lit up at the sight of Charles.

"Ha! Charlee. Welcome. Come, sit beside me and smoke a pipe or two. Tell me your news. How did you fare with the wagon-train?"

Charles sat near to Bear-Paw on the buffalo robe. He took the pipe which the brave offered him.

"The news I have is not good; that is not good for me. They would not listen to me on the wagon-train. Your war-party must have attacked them by now."

The Indian removed his pipe from his mouth and chuckled.

"I told you so Charlee. The 'white-eyes' are fools. You waste your time on them. Come, my squaw cooks the meal, we will smoke our pipes together in peace until she is ready."

They smoked in silence while Bear-Paw's number two squaw bustled around seeing to the interior arrangements of the tipi. She was much younger than 'Sweet Prairie Blossom,' about eighteen years old. She had not been long married and was full of life and fun. She and Charles got along very well together and they enjoyed a bit of flirting unbeknown to Bear-Paw and, so they believed, his other wife.

Little Song-Bird was her name, she was very good-looking with a nice figure, a very pleasant face and nicely formed legs. As she passed by Charles in the course of her duties she gave him encouraging glances which were not lost on him; he had been through this before with her.

'Sweet Prairie Blossom' now brought in the food she had prepared and her husband and Charles began to eat. They ate in silence for the most part until all the meal had been consumed. With a satisfied grunt Bear-Paw wiped his mouth and reached for his pipe once more. Charles took the opportunity to move away slightly so as to be not so noticeable to him.

Bear-Paw was a fine looking brave of about thirty-eight or so, getting near the veteran stage. He was well muscled and tall; not so tall as Charles though. He was well known for his prowess in battle and for his quick temper.

He smoked his pipe peacefully enough, a far away look in his eyes as he digested his meal and let the fragrance of his pipe's contents take control of his faculties.

'Little Song Bird' now took the opportunity to get some attention from Charles. She passed by him very provokingly swinging her hips gently as she did so. The result was just as she hoped and expected. Charles put out a hand and patted her on the bottom. Bear-Paw failed to notice anything amiss. As she returned she received another pat on her bottom. Charles was enjoying himself. This procedure continued for some time as the young squaw found all kinds of excuses to pass to and fro close to Charles. Sometimes she received a caress of her legs or, one occasion, her thigh. She didn't seem to mind, in fact she enjoyed it. Bear-Paw was too far gone with his pipe to notice anything wrong. Charles kept a wary eye upon him just the same. Any 'funny business' with either of his squaws would call forth his wrath. A killing and a scalping would follow, friend or no friend.

At length Bear-Paw shook himself and returned from his dream world to reality. The two guilty parties immediately assumed complete innocence. Charles glanced at 'Sweet Prairie Blossom', she was looking at him grimly; he understood straight away. He felt himself going red in the face; she had seen his performance with the young squaw! Would she tell her husband? Charles stared at her for a few moments trying to read her thoughts. She didn't approve of his behaviour that he surmised; he dropped his gaze. He wished he didn't blush so much, Bear-Paw would notice for sure.

Just then a commotion outside drew his attention.

"Sounds like the war-party has returned," he remarked.

Bear-Paw nodded.

"Make much noise, take many scalps; maybe get prisoners too."

Charles was not in the mood to linger much longer; as soon as he could he made his excuses and left. Bear-Paw resumed his pipe. Once outside the tipi Charles prepared to go and see what the war-party had brought in the way of booty. He was stopped by 'Sweet Prairie Blossom'.

"Charlee," she said, "Bear-Paw would be angry if he knew you had looked upon his squaw with longing and lust in your eyes. Don't deny it. I have seen you not only this time but many times before. I have longed to tell Bear-Paw, but no! I thought it will not last. To-day I saw that I was mistaken. What do you say?"

Charles was taken aback by her attack; he had thought his little flirtation had gone unnoticed, now it seemed Bear-Paw would be informed. Charles well knew how the Sioux took these matters seriously.

"I'm sorry 'Prairie Blossom', he said, " do you have to tell Bear-Paw? It will mean the end of his friendship with me. Do you want that to happen?"

'Sweet Prairie Blossom' shook her head.

"No Charlee, your friendship must continue. No more lusting after 'Song Bird'. That must stop. You need a squaw of your own."

Charles made a face.

"No thanks. I'm not yet ready for that. Maybe someday soon, but not yet."

"You ought to take squaw, Charlee. You old enough; nearly too old. Squaws will not want you pretty soon. You will have to take the 'left overs'."

She said her farewells then and Charles went towards the cluster of tipis wherein he knew he would find a group of Sioux who would gamble at cards or dice.

He had been pretty lucky so far in his gambling with the Sioux, perhaps his luck would continue; they were bound to be in a good mood after their success with the wagon-train. Most of them would be under the influence of alcohol as well.

It was dark when Charles left the gambling school; he was in a foul mood for he had lost heavily to the Indians. They had not been as heavily under the influence of alcohol as he had hoped, in fact they seemed to be hardly affected by drink at all. Anyway he had lost and they mocked him unmercifully. He had originally been the proud possessor of many blankets; not any more. A mere dozen or so were left to him now, and some of those were not of the better quality. His second rifle had also been gambled away , also his second pony. He would have surely lost much more had he not quit at last. In the morning he knew, the braves would call at his tipi to collect their winnings. No chance of fobbing them off with inferior blankets, they were too shrewd to be taken in. There was nothing else for it he would just have to grin and bear it. To think how he had won so many times against the same braves!

Charles was sure there had been some skulduggery with the cards and dice. Nothing he could accuse anyone with, but nevertheless he felt it in his bones. Damn the Sioux!

How they had laughed as the 'white-eyes' lost again and again. He sighed; it would be a long time before he gambled with them again. He had no squaw to make him more blankets, he couldn't ask 'Prairie Blossom' nor her sister 'Little Song Bird' he would just get a lecture on the evils of gambling.

With such thoughts occupying his mind Charles wended his way to his tipi, as he approached it he paused; there was someone in it. He could sense their presence. He approached the tipi cautiously. There was no sound from it, and yet his senses told him it was occupied. A year with the Sioux had sharpened those senses until he could smell and hear almost as well as they. Someone was in his tipi; they were making no sound. He crept nearer his senses alert for anything which might give him a clue as to who was in the tipi. Whoever it was they were making no movements, just standing there waiting for him. Who could it be? Surely not 'Little Song Bird'? No, she wouldn't be so foolish. Bear-Paw? That was it! He had learnt of Charles' flirtations with his squaw and was waiting in ambush to kill and scalp him. Prairie Blossom must have told him; instinctively Charlie's hand went down to his holster. There was no gun! His left hand slid downwards to his Bowie knife; it was not there!

He recalled then how he had deposited them in his tipi before visiting Bear-Paw.

He was defenceless; nothing else for it but to boldly enter the tipi and trust to luck and hope that he could defend himself before Bear-Paw struck.

Accordingly he entered the tipi rather abruptly and immediately sprang to one side so as not to be silhouetted against the light from the entrance flap.

Inside it was dark, only a faint glow from the fire. He could just make out the outline of a figure standing a few feet away. The stranger didn't move or utter a sound.

Charles waited a moment or two; this couldn't be Bear-Paw, he would have struck by now. Carefully, keeping a wary eye on the stranger, he poked the fire with the toe of his boot. It flared up after a few seconds and by its light he could see his uninvited guest.

It was the girl from the wagon-train, Sarah!

Chapter 3   The Squaw.

SHE STOOD THERE motionless her face tear-stained, her limbs trembling. Charles stared at her in disbelief.

"What the hell are you doing here?" He demanded.

"An Indian told me to stay here and not to move, if I didn't do as I was told he would return and scalp me. I've been standing here for hours. You won't scalp me will you mister, please?"

She sobbed as she said this; Charles continued to stare at her. At last he spoke.

"What in tarnation am I supposed to do with you?"

She said nothing, only continuing to sob. Charles did some thinking, at length he said,

"Was there just one Indian or were there more?"

"There was just the one warrior but he had a female with him. She seemed to give the orders. She couldn't speak English; the warrior could a little."

Charles nodded; it was as he suspected. 'Sweet Prairie Blossom!'

'Drat her,' he thought , 'she has wished a squaw upon me; revenge for flirting with her young sister. Now what am I going to do?'

"It seems to me young lady", he said, " that I'm going to have to take you as my squaw."

"I don't want to be your squaw or anybodies. Please let me go," was the reply.

Charles saw that he would have some explaining to do. He studied the girl once more.

She was not bad looking at all; somewhat smaller than he with nice shiny black hair and a nice figure. Her face was pleasant and her eyes were gray when they weren't bloodshot from weeping. She was wearing the blue dress still, it was now full length and not rolled up to her knees.

"Look here," he began, "you've been given to me as a kind of present, like it or not. When an Indian gives a present you accept it, whether you want it or not.

He would feel insulted if you refused his gift and I don't want to insult any Indian, least of all a Sioux. If I refused to accept you do you know what would happen to you?

You would be scalped and killed or maybe you would be used as a slave, at the beck and call of every brave and squaw in the village. You would have no rights at all. You might still be scalped and killed when they got tired of you. Do you understand?"

The young lady was still defiant;

"Well, I'll run away as soon as I get a chance."

Charles was not impressed.

"The Sioux would soon track you down," he said, "do you have any idea whereabouts you are? Where is the nearest town or army station? You don't know, do you? You would wander about the plains until the Sioux found you; then they would work their pleasure on you. You go ahead and run away if you still have a mind to. I won't be able to help you if you do."

She commenced weeping again. Charles began to feel some pity for her; he put his arms around her and tried to comfort her.

"Tell me your name, dear," he said.

She wiped away her tears, not very successfully, and said,

"My name is Sarah Wilson; Mrs Sarah Wilson."

"You're married! Where is your husband? Was he killed in the attack on your wagon?"

She shook her head.

"No he wasn't killed. I had a baby a few years ago, it was a girl. She lived only three months or so and then took a chill and died. My husband blamed me for her death and went off with some other female. He had been seeing her for some time before that, I believe. Anyway off he went with her to Chicago or some place near there. I didn't hear anything from him until just a few months ago when he filed for a divorce. He got his divorce and I decided to make a fresh start somewhere on the West coast. My friends Freda and Josephine persuaded me to join the wagon-train heading for Oregon, and you know the rest. Now they're dead, both of them; scalped and killed by these savages."

She began to weep again. Charles was silent for a few minutes, then he asked,

"How old are you, Mrs. Wilson? Too old for the Sioux, I should think."

She gulped back her tears and replied,

"You ought not to ask that question. I'm only thirty-three."

Charles nodded, just as thought.

"Too old fer the Sioux to bother with; they like their females to be around fifteen or sixteen, going up to twenty three or thereabouts. You're lucky they didn't rape you and scalp you."

The two of them stood looking at each other for a moment or two, then Charles said,

"I'm Charles Cunningham, late of the U.S. Army, I've lived with the Sioux nigh on a year now. I've got to know them pretty well; I know and respect their customs and I speak their lingo fairly fluently. If you're going to be my squaw you better start to learn fast. I managed alright without a squaw but it seems I got one now. The first thing you have to do is to look after the fire there. Never let it die out, winter or summer it burns all the time, understand? Well it's pretty low now so put some wood on it; the wood-pile is over there."

She hesitated, then, making up her mind she went over the wood-pile, picked some pieces of wood, and placed them on the fire.

Charles watched her performance, then he said,

"Now put some buffalo chips on the fire. You'll find them right next to the wood-pile."

Sarah crossed to the wood-pile once more, located a dark mass which she took to be the buffalo chips and picked up one; she grimaced as she did so.

"Why this is --------"

"I know very well what it is," Charles interrupted, " just put it on the fire then get another one and put it on also."

She did as ordered very reluctantly, pulling a face as she did so.

"Darn it," he exclaimed, "don't just drop it on; place it carefully. That's better, you don't want the fire to burn up too soon. This has to last us through the night. Now go and wash your hands, there's water in the jug over there. No! No not that one, darn it. That's drinking water; the other one."

Sarah did as requested swilling her hands pretty thoroughly. She looked at him helplessly.

"Do I have to be your squaw? Can't you see your way to letting me go, please?"

Charles explained once again, patiently why this was not a good idea. She listened but remained unconvinced.

Charles began to undress, preparing for his bed; Sarah watched him with some fear and dismay.

"Where do I sleep?" She asked.

Charles indicated the extra bed near his. It consisted of a buffalo robe for a blanket with another one as a kind of ground-sheet, and a pillow of doe skin stuffed with some soft material. She was relieved to some extent, at least he didn't want her to sleep with him, not yet at any rate. She was used to sleeping rough from her experience in the wagon-train so the buffalo robes and the doe skin pillow didn't bother her too much.

Charles, having by this time got himself into his bed, now turned himself to contemplate her.

"Better take off that dress; you won't want it to get creased and stained. Put it over there with my things."

Sarah was a little dismayed by this.

"But that will leave me in my underclothes," she exclaimed, "I couldn't do that."

"Suit yourself," was the reply, "it don't mean much to me. I just thought you might not to like getting your dress all messed up."

Sarah considered this, then, making up her mind, she took off her dress and deposited it where Charles had indicated originally. She got into bed hastily after that.

Sleep was long in coming; she thought over the events of the day. How she wished that she and the others had listened to Charles' warnings. Now they were all dead, most of them anyway. She shuddered when she thought about the fate of those few who weren't killed outright. She began to weep when thoughts of her friends, Freda and Josephine came into her head.

Sarah slept fitfully for ages it seemed to her; just as she fell deeply asleep she was awakened by someone pulling the blanket from her and kicking her in the ribs. She sat up abruptly. Charles was bending over her. She shrieked thinking that he was about to assault her. Instead he spoke to her in a rather sharp manner.

"Wake up lazy bones! You should be up by now and seeing to the needs of the tipi.

Go and fetch fresh drinking water. After that collect wood for the fire. You can then cook breakfast for the two of us. Go on now! The other squaws will be there before you."

Sarah looked out of the tipi.

"Why," she exclaimed, "it's still dark."

"Yeah," was the reply, "it's still dark, but pretty soon it will be light. Dawn is nigh. Take that jug and fetch some water. Not that one, stupid! The other one. Go to the river and get water. You can do that can't you? The pony herd waters down-stream; you get the water from up-stream, understand? If any squaws are bathing or washing clothes you go up-stream from them to get the water. Go along now, the squaws will all have finished before you start."

Sarah took the jug and lifted the flap of the tipi; she paused.

"Whereabouts is the river?" She asked.

Charles gave a sigh, and replied in an exasperated voice:

"Go out of the tipi, turn right and go straight on. You'll recognise the river when you come to it. Get along and don't fall in."

Sarah followed his directions and came to the river. There was a number of squaws there getting water and bathing themselves in some cases. The river was quite wide and sluggish. She filled her jug and started back feeling rather self-conscious in her state of undress. The jug which had been easy to carry when empty was now very heavy. Perhaps she ought not to have filled it so much.

She watched the other squaws; some were much younger than she, mere slips of girls she thought, several looked much older. They were all carrying their water jugs with obvious ease. She struggled with hers. Nevertheless she carried it with some difficulty, but she managed. Then she discovered that she was lost. Where was the tipi? They all looked alike to her. She tried to retrace her steps but she didn't know how far she had come. The sides of the tipis were covered with pictures of one sort or another, but she hadn't noticed what was on the side of Charles' tipi, and now she was lost. She wandered hopefully about but there didn't seem to be any obvious clues as to the whereabouts of Charles' tipi. What was she to do?

A young Sioux girl was approaching and she spoke to Sarah.

"Charlee tipi?" She said.

Sarah nodded, not knowing a word of Sioux, that was all she could think of.

The Sioux girl now spoke again, her vocabulary being obviously limited.

"Come, white-eyes," was all she could manage.

Sarah followed her back to Charles' tipi. She was so glad to get back safely that she didn't mind his being cross at her taking so long. He spoke a few words in Sioux to the girl before she left; Sarah of course had no idea what he said. The girl smiled and departed.

"What the hell kept you?" Charles demanded. He was annoyed.

"I'm sorry. I got lost."

Charles voiced his disgust.

"Well, now you've got the water, how about making me something to eat. Or is that beyond you? You'll find some food over there, it's not much but it will have to do. Later I'll go and hunt, maybe I'll get a small deer or antelope. You will have to skin it if I do."

Sarah found the food and commenced to prepare breakfast. She managed to get a fire going outside the tipi using a burning ember from the fire within. They shared the food between them. When it was all finished Charles arose from his sitting position on the ground and announced his intention of going hunting. Sarah waited for him to invite her along; it might give her a chance to escape. There was no such luck; she had other duties to do. She had to collect fire-wood and after that to see if she could pick berries from the bushes nearby. Then she had to tidy the tipi and await her lord's pleasure.

Charles was quite a while with his hunting, eventually returning with a small antelope which he had shot. He dropped it outside the tipi and called Sarah to come and skin it. She came, but had to confess that she had no idea how to skin the animal. Charles was less than pleased. Anyhow he commenced the skinning himself calling upon Sarah to watch carefully.

"As my squaw you should know how to do these things," he told her.

Over the next few weeks Sarah learnt many things which she had never thought she would have to do. Eventually she became a passably good squaw. Charles was rather pleased with her although he wouldn't show it. He obtained some squaw clothes from somewhere which fitted her quite well; a dress, leggings, blouse and moccasins. She looked very well in them. Then she turned her hands to dress-making. With a needle made from a buffalo bone and thread from animal skins she began to make dresses and moccasins for herself.

She was also able to repair Charles' clothes too. She had to work hard though at other things such as making containers for water and food and learning to use every bit of the buffalo. There were arrows to make and blankets to replace the ones Charles had lost at cards. She had to rise early, very early, in the mornings to fetch water and fire-wood. There was food to prepare for Charles, woe betide her if his meals were not ready on time. Many other tasks were required of her most of which she was not used to; there was little time to herself which perhaps was not such a bad thing as it gave her little opportunity to think about her dead friends from the wagon-train.

There was one thing which bothered her a little as the weeks went by; that was her relationship with Charles. She was quite attractive she knew, the Sioux life had not spoilt her looks, if anything it had enhanced them. She was now nicely tanned all over. Not as deeply tanned as a Sioux but very nearly. Charles, however, didn't seem to notice. That wasn't quite true, she admitted, he had noticed and admired, but had done nothing about it.

The thing which intrigued her was that young Indian girl; the one who had helped her when she had got lost. Well, she was a fairly frequent visitor to their tipi. She never entered but stood outside talking to Charles. Almost every day. On the days when she didn't come Charles would be missing for an hour or so. Sarah was of the opinion that he then called upon her. She began to feel a little jealous as, although she couldn't understand a word of what they said, it was quite obvious to her that they were in love. She resolved to tackle Charles about it. One day, after the girl had called and Charles was in a good mood, she broached the subject.

"Who is that girl? She seems to call quite a lot. She seems to be very attractive, don't you think so?"

Charles seemed a little surprised by her sudden attack. He stared at her for a few minutes, then he said,

"She is a friend of mine. Yes, she is very attractive. Her name is 'Little White Bird.'"

"That seems a nice name. How old is she? She seems very young to me."

"She would seem young to you; after all you are thirty-three, too old for the Sioux to consider as a wife," Charles replied somewhat snappily.

Sarah was hurt by this reply and subsided into silence for a few hours. She would try again some other time when he was perhaps in a better mood. The young girl's visits continued as before.

Chapter 4   Princess.

SARAH'S OPPORTUNITY WAS a long time in coming, Charles kept her busy about the tipi. The buffalo herd was thinning out as more and more of the animals departed for new grazing grounds. The Sioux decided to hold one more buffalo hunt before moving their village to a more lucrative spot.

Charles announced their intention to Sarah.

"You'll have to skin the buffalo I kill,"he informed her.

She took this news with considerable dismay.

"Oh, but I don't know how to skin a buffalo," she said.

"I'm well aware of that,"Charles replied, "Bear-Paw's squaws will help you and show you how to do it. They will skin the buffalo he kills first, then they will lend a hand with ours. You help them, not that they will need any help, it will give you some idea of what you have to do."

Sarah turned a little sulky; she would get her dress blood-stained she was sure. Just when she imagined Charles might admire it too.

For the buffalo hunt Charles had borrowed a Buffalo-gun. This had been taken by a Sioux warrior from a buffalo hunter. It was the usual Sharps single-shot weapon of 0.5inch.calibre. A big powerful weapon. The Sioux had tried it without much success and they were interested to find out what Charles could do with it. The rest of them would use the traditional methods of arrow and lance.

The next day the braves went out to the buffalo herd and began the hunt. They rode amongst the herd shooting their arrows into them, the buffalo began to drop. The herd took no notice but went on grazing. Charles took his position nearby and set up his buffalo-gun. He had a long forked stick which he stuck in the ground and then balanced the gun barrel on it. He was then able to keep the gun steady while he took aim. Selecting a buffalo about a hundred yards away he took aim and fired. The buffalo dropped. Charles reloaded his gun and tried for a buffalo further away, some three hundred yards or thereabouts. The result was the same; another dead buffalo.

By this time the herd was getting restless, still they showed no interest in what was happening. The hunt was just about over now, the Sioux were satisfied with the buffalo they had killed. The braves departed leaving their squaws to butcher the dead animals and transfer their remains to the village. Now, at last, the herd began to take fright and a stampede took place. Charles joined with his friend 'Bear-Paw' and went back to the village. There, after leaving their ponies with the rest of the pony herd, they went to 'Bear-Paw's' tipi and smoked a pipe.

Their squaws were a long time coming, Charles expressed some anxiety about this; his companion reassured him.

"Squaws good. Bye and bye bring buffalo to tipi. Help your squaw first, Charlee. She needs much help. You beat her Charlee; she soon learn then."

Charles thanked him for his advice; beat Sarah! Well it bore thinking about. She had much to learn and was pretty slow about it; beat her! Well, he would consider the matter. Let's see what she has done with the buffalo first. Buffalo steak for supper would be very nice.

As it happened Sarah made a good supper for him and thus saved herself from a possible beating.

"Charles", she said, after she had cleared away the supper things and had washed them, "tell me more about your friend, Little White Bird."

Charles looked suspiciously at her;

"Why the interest in her? She has nothing to do with you. However, if you really want to know, she is a Shaman. You know what that is?"

Sarah did know, she had heard the word before.

"It means," she said, "that she has medicine. She is a medicine man. How strange."

Charles made an impatient gesture.

"It means that she is sacred to the Sioux. She has medicine as you say but that does not mean she can heal things. Her medicine is spirtual. She can interpret dreams. She has dreams herself, not the stupid dreams of ordinary folk, but dreams full of meaning.

The Sioux are a spiritual people. They worship the Great Spirit or 'wakan'. Little White Bird is a 'Wicasa-Wakan' or holy one. Making medicine in her case means invoking the Sacred Powers. Medicine is sought through prayer, visions and ritual. The sacred circle, as the perfect form and the shape of natural phenomena such as the sun, is represented by the camp circle and the base of the tipi. Little White Bird is untouchable by me and by the Sioux warriors. She is forbidden to marry as long as she receives visions from 'wakan'"

Sarah received this information with some surprise; so Charles could never marry the Sioux girl while she was receiving dreams or visions supposedly sent by the Great Spirit. How amusing! No wonder Charles was frequently in a bad mood.

"Tell me about her dreams Charles, please. It might help me to understand better."

Charles hesitated, then he said,

"Her dreams are full of meaning for her people. A little while ago, for instance she had a vivid dream which she interpreted as meaning the buffalo would soon be scarce and it showed her where to find a large herd of them. The Sioux moved the whole village to the spot indicated in her dream and a few days later a large buffalo herd came. The same herd we hunted to-day."

"But surely," Sarah objected, "that could have been mere coincidence; or maybe she got information some other way."

Charles shook his head; "You're sceptic, I can tell. There have been other instances of her dreams or visions helping her tribe in other ways. The Sioux believe her anyway and so do I."

"I thought that being a white man you wouldn't believe such superstions. Am I wrong? Have you left behind all your religion? Did you have any religion in the first place? You took me as your squaw without much fuss."

Charles looked annoyed.

"I had plenty of religion; still have. I had a Christian upbringing. Living amongst the Sioux I have come to respect their beliefs and they respect mine. Taking you as my squaw saved your life as I've tried to tell you several times. It was no choice of mine.

The Sioux have come to trust me and I don't want to do anything to upset them. I have been able to help them on a couple of occasions, telling them how to avoid the cavalry patrols. I speak their language pretty fluently as you know. It took me a long time but I managed it."

Sarah was silent; this was a long speech for Charles as she knew. Maybe there was something in what he said. She would have to think about it.

Shortly after they turned in; an early rise in the morning as usual for Sarah.

After breakfast the following morning Sarah started her daily chores, she was becoming used to them now. What had formerly been hard, unremitting work, was now much more easy for her. She still harboured considerable resentment though. All those braves just lounging around doing nothing except gamble and spin yarns about their sexual conquests with other squaws than their own. Charles was no better, although he didn't indulge in sexual stories, or did he? He'd better not tell tales about her! The very idea!

As usual the Sioux girl made her appearance looking as young and as fresh as ever. Sarah could not help but admire her lovely figure and her pleasant face. Nice long shiney black hair and nicely shaped legs. She was wearing a dress which came down to her knees allowing a good deal of her legs to be exposed. They were very nice and beautifully copper coloured as was the rest of her. A pair of moccasins encased her pretty feet. She greeted Charles enthusiastically, and he returned the greeting just as enthusiastically. Then they fell into conversation, chatting away for ages it seemed like to Sarah. At last the young girl took her leave leaving Charles to gaze after her longingly.

Sarah turned to her chores which she had neglected while she watched the two conversing together. This did not go unnoticed by Charles.

"Hey! Lazy squaw! Attend to your work. Don't bother listening to our conversation, you can't understand it anyway."

Sarah bent to her tasks; that was what Charles thought. He didn't dream that she had began to understand some Sioux. Not enough to converse with, but enough to get the gist of his conversation with 'Little White Bird'.

After her tasks were almost completed for the day she asked Charles about the girl once more.

"It's a shame that you cannot marry. She would suit you better than I. Why don't you both elope? You could be away from here before anyone discovered it I'm sure."

"She wouldn't go. I suggested it once. No the Princess is devoted to her people and the Great Spirit."

"Princess! Is that her real status? Or is that just your name for her? She is lovely enough to be a princess."

Charles laughed;

"I call her Princess because she is so lovely. I don't think she would know what a real princess is."

Sarah found her work fairly easy once she had got used to it. There was one part of it though that she found hard and that was the dressing of skins from the animals which Charles had killed. The skins of the antelope and deer she didn't mind so much, but the buffalo hides were a different matter. This involved the cleaning, curing, scraping and tanning of very heavy hides; very arduous indeed. Then she had to convert them into useable articles.

Sarah wracked her brains to find some way around this work. Charles let it be known to her that he expected her to do this work without complaint. It was the usual work of a squaw. Beading and quilling Sarah could manage easily with a little practice.

Chapter 5   Winter.

THE YEAR WAS far spent now and soon the Sioux would be looking for winter quarters. Charles mentioned this to his squaw. Sarah wondered what that would entail.

"You will have to dismantle the tipi and transport it to wherever we go for the winter," he informed her.

"Oh, don't we live in the tipi then?" She asked.

Charles replied, somewhat impatiently,

"Oh course we live in the tipi; you have to erect it at our new camping grounds.Don't take too long about it either; it gets cold hanging around."

'Lazy hound' Sarah thought. As if he couldn't lend a hand. That was the way of the Sioux she knew very well. Women do all the work. She conveniently overlooked the fact that the men did all the hunting and fighting; very dangerous pastimes both of them. That was the reason that the Sioux had several wives; the men tended to die comparatively young and therefore there was a surplus of women. Mutiple marriages gave all the women a chance to have children.

Two or more wives made such tasks as moving and erecting the tipi less arduous

Sarah knew all this but was not in the mood for argument. She had the problem of dressing the buffalo skins and was not looking forward to it. She had made a start but was growing weary of her task; Charles was growing impatient with her. All at once she found a solution.

Two young girls, about twelve or thirteen years of age, came nosing around her tipi one day. They were curious to see what a 'white-eyes squaw' could do. Sarah soon commandeered them into helping her with the dressing of the buffalo hides. She was pleasantly surprised to find them willing and skilful. The work progressed smoothly.

In a few days it was complete and Charles was surprised and pleased.

"Just shows what you can do,"he said, "especially when you give your mind to it."

Sarah said nothing, but she gave the two girls some bright buttons and bangles which she had acquired from Charles. They were delighted and promised to help Sarah with other chores.

The whole village now prepared to move to winter quarters; 'Little White Bird' had seen in a dream the place to which they should go. Sarah was, as usual, sceptical.

"I hope she knows what she's doing," she complained.

Charles said nothing, he knew Sarah too well by now; he also knew 'Little White Bird' as well and had complete confidence in her.

Dismantling the tipi was a struggle for Sarah until her two young helpers arrived. With their assistance the task was soon accomplished. The tipi poles were packed onto a pony which Charles had provided, the rest of their belongings were carried on the ponies which they were to ride. The whole village moved off once everyone was ready. Charles rode in front with the rest of the males while Sarah rode in the rear with the females. They set off early in the morning and travelled all day. With the onset of evening they pitched camp near a stream and prepared to spend the night under the stars. Sarah was not too pleased with this but had to put up with it.

"Confound that girl,"she said, " you would think she could dream of a place a little nearer at hand so we could pitch our tipi and spend the night in comfort."

She slept well, nevertheless, and awoke in the early morning feeling well rested.

The following day they resumed their journey until early in the afternoon they arrived at a suitable place to pitch their tipis. The girls were on hand to help Sarah and so the tipi was erected without much bother. It was to remain so until the winter was over.

Sarah rewarded the Sioux girls with coloured ribbons and bright metal buttons. They were well pleased. Life followed the usual pattern for a few days until Charles decided to hunt the buffalo again. The whole village turned out for the hunt, probably the last one of the year. Charles killed his buffalo and left Sarah to skin it and to transport it back to the tipi. This she did with considerable help from her two young assisstants.

Charles was surprised to say the least when the buffalo appeared at the entrance to the tipi.

"Well I'm darned," he exclaimed, "how in hell did you manage that? You must have had some help. Bear-Paw's squaws couldn't have helped, they were too busy with their own buffalo, besides 'Little Song Bird' is pregnant.'"

Sarah smirked;

"Surprised you did I? Well I did have some help. About time too. You expect far too much from me, Charles. I had the help of two young girls; they helped with the tipi too. You didn't think I erected it all by myself, did you?"

Charles was surprised; he asked about the girls and what rewards they were given for their assisstance. Sarah told him.

"Well, I'm damned," he said, "you're not as helpless as I thought. Well done Sarah. What are you aiming to do when your supply of buttons and ribbons is finished?"

"You can get me some more. Win them at cards or dice. You like to gamble with the redskins. Now you can turn it to some use; help your squaw a little."

Sarah found the winter weather very trying, as the year drew to a close so it became colder and colder. She was still required to rise early in the mornings and fetch wood and water. There was no lingering in bed just because it was cold. She found the tipi surprisingly warm though. After performing her household duties she would snuggle down in the tipi and keep warm; that is until Charles came in and roused her. One of her duties, an unpleasant one she considered, was to keep a supply of 'buffalo chips'

in the tipi to put on the fire; they burnt rather well and were a good and easily obtained fuel. Easily obtained they might be in the warmer months but not as easily obtained now.

"Hugh!" She said, "buffalo chips indeed. Why it's nothing more than shit; buffalo shit. I'm expected to collect it with my bare hands too!"

"Yeah, well it makes good fuel for the fire, shit or no shit. Don't you forget; don't let the fire go out. It's a damn good beating for you if you do."

Sarah sniffed, she wasn't going to let any fire go out, not in this weather any way.

Charles grinned,

"There's a good girl. Don't pick any soft ones will you? Remember to collect only the hard ones; the ones which have been passed a few hours ago."

The winter proved to be a severe one, several of the old people died despite what the younger members of the tribe could do for them. One or two babies died too. There was snow from December onwards, very little in the way of buffalo hunting could be done; a few antelope and small deer formed the main source of food for many weeks. Sarah and Charles suffered in this respect almost as much as the Sioux; Charles usually did manage to kill something for the pot most days.

'Little White Bird' still came to see Charles though not as frequently as before, she too was feeling the cold. Charles didn't go to see her so often for the same reason.

Sarah was beginning to feel like a real squaw except for one thing. Her actual relationship with Charles was not satisfying her; she wanted more from it. She decided to put him to the test.

One night when they were each snug in their respective beds she said,

"I'm awful cold Charles laid here by myself. Could I possibly come closer to you?"

Charles grunted; she took this as an affirmative and moved her bed and blankets nearer to him. Very near, in fact. She settled herself with a contented sigh. There was silence for a while; no reaction from Charles. Sarah tried again.

"This is better, don't you think so? I'm so much warmer now. Charles do you think I'm attractive? I used to think so, but I'm not so sure now."

Now this was a lie as she had contemplated herself in her reflection in the stream from which she obtained the water. She had looked very nice in her Sioux blouse and leggings. She was, she felt, very desirable. Surely Charles would think so too. Perhaps he was too taken with the young Sioux girl, his Princess as he called her. She was very beautiful, no doubt, but unobtainable for the present. In the meantime Sarah was his squaw, at least in name. He growled at her.

"What in hell are you doing? Of course you are attractive; very attractive. Now settle down and go to sleep."

She rolled over until she was almost on top of him. He was almost naked as was she. She kissed him on his lips. Startled, he sat upright. She put her arms around him and held him tightly.

"Oh! Charles! Keep me warm, please. You say I am very attractive; well do something about it!"

He was surprised at this request. For a few moments he was at a loss what to do; he soon recovered from his surprise.

"Idiot girl! Are you sure about this? You are? Well we'll see."

Suiting action to the words he kissed her passionately on her lips and rolled over on top of her. What followed was sheer bliss for Sarah. She felt wanted as a woman once again. It was a bit painful at first for she hadn't had intercourse since her husband left her. When it was all over she sighed with contentment. Charles rolled off her and lay breathing heavily.

"That was wonderful. Was it the same for you?"

Charles agreed; it had been wonderful for him too.

"Now get to sleep or I won't be answerable for what I might do," he replied.

Sarah settled herself then, not without some thoughts of pestering him again; it had been somewhat painful though and she decided to follow his advice and go to sleep.

At the crack of dawn she was up and away out to the river. There she collected water and bathed. There was ice on the water and she had to break it; the water was deliciously cold and refreshing. On the way back to the tipi she collected fire-wood from the broken branches of the trees. Charles was waiting for her; he was still abed.

"Where have you been? You've taken your time. Get breakfast ready, put some buffalo chips on the fire."

Sarah did as she was bid. The breakfast didn't take long to get ready. Charles arose from his bed and partook of his share of food. After he went to the river where he washed and bathed himself, returning feeling much fresher.

"What was all that about last night? Fool woman! You shouldn't start that unless you are serious. Are you serious?"

"Yes, Charles, I'm serious. It's about time we did something like that. Living together like we was married.

It ain't right. It's more than a body can stand. Well I've stood it as long as I can and last night I persuaded you to do something about it."

Charles growled,

"So you're serious eh. Well you better watch your step, next thing you know we'll be having a papoose about the tipi."

Sarah had thought of that.

"Oh, no need to worry about that Charles. I made sure it would be alright for now. We can do it again to-night if you want."

Charles was not at all sure what she meant by that, still if she said it would be alright he supposed it would be.

That night was very much like the previous one. Sarah was satisfied; she would have a break from all the sexual activity and give Charles a rest; besides which she still found it a little painful.

The winter seemed slow in passing, the nights were long and dreary and the mornings were cold and damp. The tipi was as warm as ever though; it was marvellous thought Sarah, she had never before thought of a tipi as being so comfortable in the cold months. Several other tribes of Sioux, Cheyenne and Arapaho were encamped around about, the Ogallala heard of a band of Brule Sioux being attacked by the soldiers sometime just before Christmas. As usual the soldiers had killed many squaws and children, few warriors. The survivors had taken refuge in a Sans Arc village where they were made welcome and given food and shelter. Sarah wondered if the Ogallala would be attacked next.

"I think there's small chance of that," said Charles, "I picked out this spot carefully. I am pretty sure the cavalry won't find us here. It's the wrong place for us to be, they won't even think of looking here."

Sarah was surprised at this.

"How could you know this? I thought your friend 'Little White Bird' selected this place. That's true isn't it?"

Charles chuckled;

"Little White Bird dreamed her dreams and selected a suitable place, but I influenced her more than somewhat. My army experience told me where the cavalry were most likely to look."

"Do you mean to tell me that you interfered with the Great Spirits intentions? Your 'Little White Bird' is a fraud. You are the one who guides her. Dreams and visions my foot! Charles Cunningham have you been misleading the Sioux all this time?"

Charles shook his head.

"No, I ain't been misleading anybody. The Princess picked a certain spot and I merely improved upon it. I didn't think the Great Spirit would mind if I helped his people a little. I've done it before. Twice I helped the Ogallala to avoid the cavalry; each time I was proved right. That's how come they trust me. My army experience has been very useful in the past and will be now, I hope."

Spring was just around the corner, but the wintry weather continued; there were other reports of cavalry attacks upon Indian villages with the usual loss of life amongst the squaws and children. The Ogallala Sioux remained safe.

Chapter 6   The Vision Quest.

As THE WINTER slowly passed and the green shoots of early Spring began to make their appearance, so the Ogallala began to think about resuming their buffalo hunting and raiding. This particular band of Ogallala Sioux were known as 'roamers'. They, and many other Indians of the Sioux and Cheyenne tribes had turned their backs on the reservations, detesting the corruption and widespread deprivation which were rife there. They preferred to live on what they considered their homelands.

The Bureau for Indian Affairs in Washington D.C. issued an ultimatum in December 1875 ordering all the 'roamers' to return to the reservations by 31 January 1876 on penalty of being considered 'hostile'.

Despite the severe weather, Indian agents were sent to notify the non-Agency

villages of the ultimatum. These 'hostiles' had sought refuge in the richest hunting grounds and had ample buffalo meat and were wealthy in horses and robes. They were well-armed with rifles and revolvers. They were defiant of the ultimatum.

On February 8th 1876, after waiting for the ultimatum deadline to expire, General Sheridan ordered his subordinate commanders, Generals Terry and Crook, to 'prepare for operations against the hostiles'.

In previous campaigns over the previous ten years these hostile bands had proved to be extremely elusive. During the summer months they were always more mobile than the Army forces and were able to scatter if closely pursued. Winter campaigns had become the established method of defeating them.

Only General Crook took the field before the end of winter. The forces under the command of General Terry, Commander of the Department of Dakota, were delayed by severe weather and also by Terry's logistical worries.

The Indian Bureau estimated that between 400 and 800 warriors were dispersed in winter camps across the Unceded Territory. That estimate was fairly accurate, but accounted only for the winter roamers; in the spring numbers would increase.

Despite blizzards and sub-zero temperatures Crook's force was heavily scouted by the hostiles, and the cattle herd was stampeded. After ten days of searching Crook came upon an Indian camp along the Powder River Valley. It was Old Bear's camp of about 110 lodges and up to 250 warriors. Six companies, about 300 men, were sent to attack the village. The Indians fled to nearby bluffs overlooking the village and began to return fire. In the face of this determined resistance the troopers were ordered to burn the camp, destroy all the stores and withdraw. Several soldiers were killed and several more wounded. One wounded trooper was abandoned. The warriors followed and managed to recapture most of their herd.

The Sioux and Cheyenne survivors of the Powder River battle were without protection from the extreme cold, and after several days of exposure they combined with Crazy Horse's camp. News of the raid spread and gave clear warning that the Army was intent upon waging total war. As the spring grass came the Indian bands continued to join together for protection.

After his failure at the Powder River it would be two months before Crook could refit his forces for another offensive. He had failed in his winter attack against a weakened foe. A summer campaign would be necessary.

Most of this was made known to Charles. The elders of the tribe consulted him about their course of action. What did the ultimatum mean?

Charles told them what it meant; give up their freedom and live on the reservation depending upon the Indian agent giving them sufficient food, no buffalo hunting; or remain free to roam the prairie, in which case the Army would endeavour to capture or kill them.

The choice was obvious to the Ogallala; they would remain free and take their chances with the soldiers. Charles advised them to join up with other bands of the Ogallala to give themselves a real chance against the Army. The chiefs and elders decided to take his advice.

As the spring wore on and the pony herds began to lose their winter coats 'Little White Bird' began to be troubled by a dream. She spoke to Charles about it.

"Charlee," she said one day soon after she began dreaming, "I am troubled. For many nights now I have had a dream. It was most real-like. In the morning I awake but cannot recall the dream. I remember it as being very vivid but no more. What it is about I am not sure, there is a lot of ponies and warriors about, but what they are doing I do not remember."

Charles listened sympathetically; he had experienced her dreams before and knew their meanings too well to be sceptical.

"What will you do, Princess? Will the dreams continue until their meaning is revealed?"

'Little White Bird' shook her head.

"I do not know Charlee. Perhaps. Perhaps not. It is difficult. To-night if I dream again I will do something about it unless the Great Spirit sends me a meaning."

"Are you sure these dreams are sent by the Great Spirit? Perhaps there might be some other cause."

'Little White Bird' was disappointed with him.

"What other cause could there be? Charlee you disappoint me; you are an unbeliever."

Charles shrugged his shoulders; he would wait and see. Maybe tonight there would be no dream.

Sarah was an interested listener to this conversation which took place just outside her tipi. As it was spoken entirely in Sioux she understood not a word of it. She was interested because the young Sioux girl seemed uneasy about something. Sarah hoped it had nothing to do with Charles. She asked him as soon as he came in.

He told her about 'Little White Bird' and her dream; the dream that she could neither remember nor understand. Sarah laughed.

"Oh Charlie," she exclaimed, "you surely don't believe all that dream nonsense, do you? I thought you were a sensible kind of man. It's all a load of nonsense, that's what it is."

Charles was not so sure about it; looking at it from a white-man's point of view he thought the same as Sarah, but he had experienced 'Little White Bird's' dreams before and he was convinced there was something in them. He kept silent. Sarah displayed her contempt for the whole thing.

Charles hunted the following day and on his way back to his tipi he met 'Sweet Prairie Blossom'.

"Ho there, Charlee," she called, "how are you? How is your squaw? Does she fulfil your expectations?

"Yes, 'Prairie Blossom' she meets my expectations. No thanks to you though. I've had a tough time breaking her in. I suppose I asked for it, flirting with your sister as I did."

Sweet Prairie Blossom grinned.

"No time for other squaws now Charlee, all your time spent with your white-eyes squaw."

Charles was not at all amused. His hopes of taking his Princess as his squaw were apparently ruined, and all thanks to 'Prairie Blossom'. He had completed the ruin when he allowed himself to make love to Sarah that night and the following night.

He silently cursed 'Prairie Blossom' as he made his way towards his tipi. She, for her part, just sniggered.

When he arrived at his tipi he was met by Sarah.

"Your little Sioux girl has been here, looking for you," she said.

Charles dropped the deer he was carrying;

"Where has she gone?" He asked.

Before Sarah could answer the girl herself appeared at the entrance to the tipi.

She conversed in the Sioux tongue as before.

"Charlee, the dream came again last night. I cannot understand it. I have consulted the shaman and know what I must do. I must go on the Vision Quest. To-morrow I go. My mother, 'Yellow Moon' goes with me. You too Charlee, come with me, please. You can protect us."

Charles was for the moment speechless. He recovered himself fairly quickly.

"Princess, you know I will go with you wherever you wish. What about my squaw?"

The Princess looked rather scornfully at Sarah.

"She stays here. No go with us. Plenty people look after her. She come to no harm"

A few more words were exchanged and then she was gone. Charles was left to explain things to Sarah.

"Vision Quest? What is this Vision Quest? An excuse to leave me and go with your Sioux squaw."

Charles explained as well as he could;

"The Vision Quest is sought by warriors who wish for spiritual guidance for their future. They take themselves off to a secluded place such as a cave or into the desert or deserted part of the prairie. There they stay, not eating or drinking, wrapped up in a blanket, or sometimes naked, until they receive a vision sent by the Great Spirit. This vision guides them through their future life. Usually only warriors take the Quest, but it is not unknown for females to take it as well. Sometimes they stay not eating or drinking for a week or more until they receive their vision."

Sarah was sceptical about the whole business.

"Why what nonsense. Not eating or drinking for a whole week. No wonder they get a vision; they hallucinate. That's all the vision is; an hallucination."

Nevertheless Charles was set upon escorting his Princess and her mother come what may. Sarah would be well looked after. She need not be lonely during his absence, the two young girls would stay with her until he returned.

So Charles and his females set out the next day, leaving Sarah with ample supply of food for a week and company at nights in the shape of those two girls.

Charles was wearing ordinary trousers and boots with a Sioux hunting shirt made for him by his Princess. She had made it several weeks ago and he had been looking for a chance to wear it; this seemed to be as good a time as any. He wore his six-gun on his right hip as usual and a Bowie knife on his left. His rifle was in a scabbard by his left leg. His saddle and blankets completed his outfit.

The two females rode bare-back as was usual with the Sioux, only a blanket between them and their horse. They were carrying a lot of extras in the way of food and fuel.

Charles smiled at this, still he reflected, they ought to know what they are doing.

On they went across the plains and into unkown territory as far as Charles was concerned. The day was warm, very warm for the time of year. There was no pause for refreshments or to breathe the horses. On they went, walking their mounts for long spells, trotting them from time to time, and once breaking into a canter.

Where they were heading Charles had no idea, the plain seemed endless, and hot. The sun was scorching; never before had Charles known such heat at that time of year.

They were headed due west towards the distant mountains, conversation was limited and then only between the two females. Charles longed to ask them where they were headed but he forebore; he would know when he got there.

The after noon was well advanced before a halt was made. Charles looked about him; the plain was fairly flat here with a few rocky outcrops and trees scattered about. It looked dry and barren otherwise. They dismounted and Charles did likewise.

'Yellow Moon' spoke to him then.

"White-eyes, here are the Sioux Sacred burying grounds. This is where 'Little White Bird' must seek her vision. No white-eyes has seen these grounds before. You must not tell where they are."

Charles promised; it would be easy as he had no idea where they were anyway. 'Yellow Moon' and her daughter began to unpack the equipment they had brought with them. Charles watched with some interest. When all was unpacked the Princess began to strip, her mother shooing him away. He retired a few paces and turned his back. After what he thought was a decent interval he turned back again. There she was, his Princess, wrapped only in a blanket waiting for him to turn around.

She looked serious.

"Charlee," she said, "I go now to find my vision. It maybe will give me the answer to my dream. Do not worry; the Great Spirit will guard me. My mother will look after you. Guard her well."

'Little White Bird' then walked a few paces forwards and began to descend; Charles was startled at this, hurrying forwards he discovered to his astonishment that they were on the edge of a large canyon. 'Little White Bird' had merely began to descend the canyon side. She continued downwards carefully, avoiding the numerous rocks and cacti. She got smaller and smaller as she went down. At last she reached the bottom and began to make her way to the other side. Charles saw, with some horror, that she had to pass numerous 'burial platforms' upon which reposed the corpses of departed braves, resting peacefully no doubt, but in various stages of decay.

The girl seemed not to mind as she walked across the canyon floor. At last she reached the other side and commenced to climb. Up she went until she found the entrance to a cave. The cave-mouth loomed black and uninviting but she entered without hesitation. Charles watched her as she disappeared into the dark interior; supposing the cave were inhabited by a mountain lion or a bear, even a wolf or rattle snake would be bad enough. He waited with bated breath. There was no sound, all was quiet. 'Yellow Moon' seated herself comfortably on the ground some distance away from the canyon side.

"Come, white-eyes," she called, "sit here and do not worry. 'Little White Bird' must fix her mind on the Great Spirit now. He will guide her and take care of her. Nothing you can do. Rest."

Charles seated himself upon the ground; he was anxious; he couldn't rest. After a few minutes he got up and paced about. The squaw watched him with some amusement, she had brought a whole bundle of moccasins, hunting-shirts and war-shirts to repair and this she proceeded to do. Eventually Charles seated himself beside her and watched the proceedings. After a while he got tired of that and decided to take a walk and see how the land lay.

Leaving the squaw to her tasks he proceeded to walk towards the open plain to the East. He walked onwards for about a mile amongst cacti and loose rocks; he saw nothing of any interest. He turned then and slowly made his way back to where 'Yellow Moon' was sitting, still busy with her mending. He noticed that the canyon was almost impossible to see until one got almost on top of it. The ground around the canyon wall was slightly risen above the level of the rest of the prairie, this was what made it difficult to see. The canyon itself was a narrow slit at its upper lip, widening out below. Charles could well understand that the Sioux burial grounds had not been discovered yet by the Army; long may this state of affairs continue!

The day was hot and quiet, nothing seemed to be stirring. Charles sighed deeply and sat down beside 'Yellow Moon.' She grunted at him and went on with her tasks. At last she put them on one side and spoke;

"The white-eyes is weary with watching 'Yellow Moon' at her work. Come! The day draws to a close. I make meal for us. Soon it will be ready. Then we sleep. You see to horses. Go now."

Charles saw to the horses, swilled his hands in a small stream nearby, and then joined his companion for the meal. She was cooking it on a small fire she had made. He had no idea what she was cooking but it smelt good. When all was ready he took his share and ate it with great relish; it not only smelt good, but it tasted good too.

After eating they spread their blankets on the ground and prepared to sleep. Charles was not too happy about sleeping in the open but 'Yellow Moon' didn't seem to mind. They slept pretty well although Charles awoke two or three times but there was nothing to disturb them, nothing at all. He was concerned about 'Little White Bird' all alone in that cave, he couldn't help it.

The next day and the day after were repeats of the first day; nothing to do for Charles and nothing stirring out on the prairie. 'Yellow Moon' went on with her mending while Charles wandered far and wide in search of signs of life.

They ate well, twice a day, the squaw cooked well and the meals were very tasty. Nothing to complain about there. However on the fourth day 'Yellow Moon' complained that the morning meal would be the last unless Charles could catch or kill something for supper. He protested that he had seen nothing to kill or catch, nothing at all. She was adamant; Charles must get something.

"Wakan, the Great Spirit," she declared, "will provide something, you will see. Trust him Charles, and go get something."

So Charles set out on his mission. He was glad to give his horse some exercise at last. The prairie was bare seemingly, no game of any kind. It was hot, unusually so at that time of year, and he was glad when he discovered a small stream where he could refill his canteen and water his horse. That accomplished, he was about to remount when he suddenly espied a young antelope not far away. It was attracted by the water, and was preparing to drink oblivious to his presence nearby. It was an easy shot for him and the animal came crashing down.

His shot echoed and re-echoed across the prairie. It could be heard for miles.

He hastily packed the animal on his horse's back and, mounting him, rode off as fast as he could. It was with a sense of relief that he arrived back at place where he had left 'Yellow Moon'. She was pleased to see him back safely but she was cross about his shooting.

"Make too much noise, Charlee. Everyone hear; soldiers hear, Crow Indians hear. Too much noise. All will know we are here."

Charles was suitably chastised. The Crow Indians were traditional enemies of the Sioux. How was he expected to kill an animal for supper without shooting it? With bow and arrow he supposed. In that case it would probably be goodbye to supper; his skill with bow and arrow was not up to it.

They made a good meal of the antelope anyway, 'Yellow Moons' cooking being up to scratch as usual. Afterwards Charles watered and fed the horses and fastened them for the night, then he and the squaw settled themselves in their blankets and went to sleep.

The next day was the fifth day of 'Little White Birds' vision quest and Charles was up very early, before 'Yellow Moon' in fact, a circumstance which didn't please her.

"You rise too early, Charlee," she said, "squaw no get water or fire-wood yet. Go back to sleep."

Charles couldn't sleep any more, he was anxious about his 'Princess'. The fifth day! Surely she will have had her vision by now? Perhaps she wasn't going to have a vision. 'Yellow Moon' became annoyed when he expressed those feelings. Of course she would have her vision, the Great Spirit would visit her and make all things clear.

The day passed slowly for Charles; the weather continued hot. As the day wore on he took to wandering again in a different direction this time. He had travelled a good mile or so when all of a sudden he sighted a dust cloud in the distance. It was easy to see across the flat plains and it was moving in his direction. He screwed up his eyes to view it more clearly; it was a cavalry patrol!

He hadn't been spotted yet, he hoped, and he made a hasty retreat towards the only cover available, a pile of rocks nearby. He crouched in their shadow hoping that the soldiers wouldn't pass too close. They didn't; they passed in fact some distance from him without a glance in his direction. That was a relief, but what about 'Yellow Moon'? She must be warned at once. Charles set off at a fast pace breaking into a run after a few yards. He arrived eventually at the camp site to find her calmly attending to her mending. She wasn't the least concerned about soldiers.

"No bother about them, Charlee. You take care about noise in future. You bit careless. 'Yellow Moon' take care of you."

They noticed the change in the weather then. The sky was clouding over and the sun was gradually being hidden by black clouds. A storm was brewing. There was a distinct chill in the air. 'Yellow Moon' found a place where they could shelter for the night for it looked as though the storm would hit them later, when they were taking their evening meal.

She had found a cave nearby amongst some boulders. Not a very big cave but enough for the two of them. A smaller cave close by did for the horses, they would be safe there. Charles and the squaw moved their things into the cave and he led the horses into the other smaller one, making sure that they were supplied with water and fodder. He joined 'Yellow Moon' in the slightly larger one. She had gone to collect as much fire-wood as she could and staggered back with her arms full. Placing it on the floor she then went out to collect some more despite Charles' protests. She returned shortly after with her arms full once more. They settled themselves on blankets spread on the cave floor. 'Yellow Moon' then built up a fire and lit it. She started to prepare the meal using the remains of the antelope Charles had killed the day before.

The storm broke just after they had finished their meal. The skies grew dark, very dark, and great fat drops of rain began to fall. Charles and 'Yellow Moon' decided to turn in as there was no prospect of doing much else. Charles checked the horses first, making sure they had sufficient water and food. He returned to the main cave to find that 'Yellow Moon' had already snuggled down amidst her blankets. She advised Charles to do likewise.

They lay in their beds listening to the rain which had now turned to a fine drizzle. Before long there was the rumble of distant thunder and the rain increased in volume.

Charles dozed , lulled by the sound of falling rain. He awoke some considerable time later to the crash of thunder almost overhead. Lightning flashed and rain fell in great torrents. The squaw continued to sleep, apparently she was not disturbed by the elements. Charles gazed at her with a certain amount of envy. How could she sleep like that with such a storm going on?

He became aware of something or someone entering the cave. The cave mouth was in darkness, the rest of the cave was illuminated feebly by the fire which had almost burnt itself out. A sudden flash of lightning illuminated the cave mouth just then. By its light Charles could make out the shape of a huge bear. It was reared up on its hind legs and was looking at him fiercely. Charles swore, and grabbed his rifle. The bear growled. 'Yellow Moon' caught hold of Charles' arm and held tightly to it.

"No shoot, white-eyes," she cried, "he is 'Wakan' the Great Spirit. He has taken upon himself the shape of a bear. No shoot!"

Chapter 7.   The Great Spirit.

"ARE YOU LOCO?" Charles asked her sharply, "The Great Spirit! That is a bear, and by the looks of it he is about ready to attack. We must be sleeping in his cave!"

"Great Spirit, no shoot Charlee!" 'Yellow Moon' repeated her warning.

The bear continued to glare at them, then, dropping down to all fours he turned and shuffled out of the cave. As he went he growled and grumbled to himself for all the world like a human-being. Charles was startled by this but could hardly stop himself from laughing. The bear continued to grumble and growl as he made his way out of the cave. Charles lowered his rifle.

"Well, if that don't beat all," he exclaimed, "He sounds almost human, grumbling like that."

'Yellow Moon' shook her head;

"I tell you Charlee, he is 'wakan' he takes upon himself the shape of a bear. In that form he has visited 'Little White Bird' and has granted her a vision. We shall hear from her in the morning."

"Bear or Great Spirit he better not have harmed her. I'll hunt him down if he has. He must have frightened her in any case appearing like that."

"White eyes no understand. By and by you will see," the squaw said.

The morning came at last and Charles decided to track the bear if he could and see where he went. He washed himself and attended to the horses first. After that he took his rifle and set about looking for bear tracks. The ground was soft after the rain and he had no difficulty finding the tracks. There they were commencing at the mouth of the cave and leading away towards the plains. Charles followed them without difficulty. The bear appeared to be on all fours at first and proceeded in this manner for about half a mile. Suddenly the pattern of the tracks changed; the bear had reared itself up onto its hind legs and walked thus for several yards. Then abruptly the tracks disappeared. It was as if he had been snatched up into thin air.

"What the hell," Charles exclaimed, "bears can't fly. Where the hell has he gone?"

He searched all around for any trace of bear or tracks; there was none. The ground was pretty hard hereabouts and tracks would be hard to find in any case. A few trees and numerous small rocks and large boulders dotted the landscape but never a trace of bear. He shook his head in disbelief and returned to 'Yellow Moon'.

She listened to his tale and laughed at him.

"No find Great Spirit, white eyes. I tell you truth; you no believe me. We shall see. Now 'Little White Bird' comes. Over there; look!"

Sure enough 'Little White Bird' was making her way slowly across the floor of the canyon; she looked tired and bedraggled. Her lovely copper-coloured features seemed a trifle pale. She began to climb the canyon face. Slowly she struggled upwards, Charles, unable to stand it any longer, rushed to help her. He had climbed half-way down the canyon side before she met him. She spoke no words to him but merely smiled. Charles assisted her to the top of the canyon without a word also. Once on level ground she spoke;

"Charlee, many thanks for your help. The Great Spirit thanks you. You look after my mother; this also has my thanks."

Charles then asked her if she had received a vision from the Great Spirit.

"Yes, Charlee. The Great Spirit came to me in the shape of a bear. He spoke to me and gave me the meaning of my dream. Now I must tell it to the Council. We go soon."

Charles was startled to hear her speak of the Great Spirit as being in the shape of a bear. Was 'Yellow Moon' right? He remained sceptical. 'Yellow Moon' looked scornfully at him as she said,

"The white-eyes no believe what I tell him. Now 'Little White Bird' tells the same. Will he believe her? White-eyes no have any belief in 'wakan'."

It took some explaining Charles decided. It was completely beyond his understanding. There had been no communication between the two females; or had there ?

They might have concocted this tale before going on the vision quest, it was quite possible. That meant that his Princess and her mother had set out to deceive him. It was unthinkable. The Princess would never do such a thing, her mother might but she would need the co-operation of her daughter. Charles was somewhat mystified by the whole business.

The journey back took longer than ever, it was getting dark before they reached the village. The two females chatted to each other but ignored Charles. He didn't mind; he had some serious thinking to do. After they had put their mounts into the horse-herd they went to their respective tipees. Before parting 'Little White Bird' spoke to Charles.

"Charlee", she said, "you look after my mother; that is good. I will remember. Now I must tell the Council about my vision. After that I tell you."

With that Charles had to be content for the time being. He didn't doubt that she would tell him everything after the Council.

Sarah was very glad to see him again; she had missed him more than she realised she would. He told her everything that had happened; she was scornful of the whole proceeding.

"She spoke to the Great Spirit who came to her in the form of a bear! Charley you surely don't believe that do you?"

"I'm not sure what to believe anymore. The Princess wouldn't deceive me knowingly. It seems far-fetched all the same. I'll wait to see what she tells the Council to-morrow."

Sarah teased him about the bear as they lay side by side in their beds that night.

Charles insisted that the animal had made grumbling noises just like a human-being. As it ambled away the noises sounded remarkably like human speech. Sarah was still sceptical.

"What did it say, then, this bear? What did it tell you? Oh, Charley you have lived with Sioux too long. You were brought up as a Christian I suppose. That is so, is it not?"

Charles agreed, he was a Christian. There were some things though which he couldn't explain; the bear incident was one of them.

The Council met the following day and debated long and seriously. When it finally broke up the day was well advanced. Charles waited impatiently for 'Little White Bird' to come to him and tell him the news. She came at last looking her best, she seemed to have recovered remarkably well from her fast. She was dressed in a white dress which came down to her knees and a pair of white moccasins. Her hair was in braids, one hanging down to her breasts on each side.

She was happy to see Charles waiting for her outside his tipee. She took him to one side and began her tale.

"Charlee,"she said, "I have told the Council what the Great Spirit revealed to me. I had dreams, very life-like dreams, but their meanings I could not understand. I remember the dreams very well but their content I could not recall. My vision quest was successful; the Grear Spirit has revealed their meaning. He showed me a scene of the pony-soldiers attacking our village in great numbers. Charlee! They were defeated! All killed, no-one left alive. Just think Charlee, all killed. I saw in my vision all their bodies lying on the ground. A wonderful victory for the Sioux!"

Charles was at a loss for words when he heard 'Little White Bird's' explanation.

"Princess" he exclaimed eventually, "you must not put too much faith in your dreams. This victory may not happen;

you may be mistaken. What does the Council intend to do?"

'Little White Bird was disappointed at his reaction. She explained further that the Council had decided to join other Sioux tribes in a big gathering not very far away. This the Great Spirit had also told her must be done. Sioux and Cheyenne would all meet at one place and await the pony soldiers.

"All white-eyes killed Charlee. All; the Great Spirit decrees."

She looked sad as she said this. A tear glistened in her eye. Charles understood.

"All white-eyes you say. Does that include me?"

'Little White Bird' nodded,

"Yes, you too Charlee. I have pleaded with the Great Spirit but it is no use. I have much sorrow."

The move took place the following day. The whole village went to a place not very far away just as the Great Spirit had ordered. There were many tribes of the Sioux already there. The Brule Sioux, the Hunkpapa Sioux, the Miniconjou Sioux, the Ogallala Sioux and the Sans Arc Sioux. The Cheyenne were there also and the Blackfoot. Hundreds of Indians and their families. Many of them had been there for several days.

The plains Indians didn't usually congregate in such numbers except for war and even then only for two or three days at a time. The warriors had families to feed and therefore they needed to hunt; either the buffalo or deer or antelope, but hunt they had to. It didn't take long to exhaust all the game in one particular area with so many hunting and so they had to move. Thus the plains Indians in such numbers couldn't afford to stay in one place for very long. It was therefore remarkable that vast numbers of them were there and had been for several days.

They were held together by the force of the personality and spirituality of one Indian; he was known as Sitting Bull.

Charles had heard of him of course but for the moment he was more interested in the place chosen for this gathering of tribes; he recognised the place alright. The Big Horn river ran nearby and this village was situated on a tributary of the Big Horn. It was the Little Big Horn and they were encamped in the Little Big Horn valley.

Chapter 8   1876 The Little Big Horn.

THE VILLAGE ON the Little Big Horn was a large one, containing all the various tribes of the Sioux and their allies. There were the Hunkpapas consisting of 260 lodges, the Ogallalas consisting of 240 lodges, the Blackfoot, Brule, and Two Kettle Sioux of 120 lodges, the Miniconjou Sioux of 150 lodges and the Sans Arc Sioux of 110 lodges. In addition to these were the Northern Cheyenne of 120 lodges and a small band of Arapahoe.

Charles had never seen so many Indians at one time, he wandered amongst the various lodges in amazement. There sure was a whole lot of Indians. Sarah accompanied him gazing about her in wonder. Many famous warriors were there and Charley pointed out some of them to his squaw.

"There is 'Sinte-Galeshka'of the Brule Sioux", he said.

Sarah gazed in bewilderment.

"What does that mean, in English?"

Charley laughed,

"I thought you could speak Sioux. It means 'Spotted Tail'".

Sarah pointed out another warrior who seemed to be rather important; a chief maybe.

Charles was enthusiastic about him;

"That is 'Crazy Horse' of the Ogallala Sioux, you should know him, he belongs to our tribe. His Sioux name is 'Tashunka Witko'. He is a great warrior with many victories over the pony soldiers."

"Strange name for a warrior,"commented Sarah.

"Not so strange as you think. 'Crazy Horse' is the name us whites have given him. It is a bad translation; it really means Wild or Untamed horse."

As they strolled around the village they suddenly came upon a group of Sioux who were gathered around a somewhat older warrior who seemed to be giving them instruction about something.

"That," Charley exclaimed, "is 'Tatanka-Yotunka' or 'Sitting Bull' mighty medicine man of the Hunkpapa. I wonder what he is telling those young men."

Sarah had not heard of him before and she was not impressed. They made their way back to their tipee. Charley was quite excited by this congregation of Indians and wondered what it was all about. His friend, 'Bear Paw' enlightened him.

"Charlee," he said, "Sitting Bull has danced the Sun Dance and has sacrificed fifty pieces of his flesh. In return he has been granted a vision by the Great Spirit. He saw, in the vision, many pony soldiers falling upside down into this village. He takes this to mean we shall have a great victory over them. What do you think?"

Charles was startled by this news; a victory over the white men, just as 'Little White Bird' had foretold, or, rather the Great Spirit had foretold. He was silent for a few moments.

"Bear Paw," he said at last, "do not put too much faith in dreams, much may happen to alter their meaning."

Bear Paw looked scornfully at his white-eye friend, an unbeliever he thought, time would tell. Let the white-eyes watch carefully and he will see.

Charles looked sadly after him as he walked away; dreams are one thing, reality is another. He took Sarah back to their tipee, she was sceptical about the whole business.

"Who ever heard of such things coming to pass? Dreams indeed! I think your friend

'Little White Bird' and this 'Sitting Bull' as you call him have put their heads together and concocted this tale of dreams and visions."

Charles protested; his Princess wouldn't do such a thing. She definitely had a vision, or thought she had. Anyhow all would be revealed in due course. In the meantime he would have to hunt the buffalo if any could be found. With all these Indians about the buffalo might be scarce.

The war department of the U.S. had decided to deal with the Indians once and for all. General Terry had been given overall command of the forces approaching the Little Big Horn from the North and North-West. He was a 49 year old veteran of the Civil War, but this was his first campaign in 11 years. He had no experience of Indian fighting. Under his command was the so-called Montana column, commanded by Colonel John Gibbon the 49 year old commander of the 7th Infantry Regiment.

Coming up from the South was another band of soldiers under the command of Brigadier General George Crook. He had experience of Indian fighting and had already fought the Sioux and Cheyenne at Powder River. He was now poised at Fort Fetterman with his men awaiting a break in the weather to allow him to advance Northwards.

Thus the Sioux and their allies were about to be caught in a two armed pincer movement. They were, however, not altogether unaware of the Army's intentions and took steps to disrupt them. Crazy Horse led a band of Sioux and Cheyenne Southwards towards Crook's army as it headed North. It had been scouted by the Indians ever since leaving Fort Fetterman. Crook had not travelled very far before he was attacked. At about 8.30am Crazy Horse and hundreds of Sioux and Cheyenne struck Crook's camp sweeping in from the north. A fierce battle ensued. Crook with about 1,000 soldiers was beaten back and suffered heavy casualties. The Indians departed after satisfying themselves that he wouldn't trouble them anymore. Crook decided to retire back to Fort Fetterman to have his wounded attended to and to refit his troops. He refused to advance any further and took no further part in the campaign.

Thus one prong of the pincer was removed.

Meanwhile General Terry had eventually linked up with Gibbon on the Yellowstone river. They marched south towards the Little Big Horn. Gibbon had under his command the 7th Cavalry, commander Lieutenant -Colonel George Armstrong Custer.

As they neared the Little Big Horn Terry detached Custer and his command to detect the Indian village if he could. Custer was given the option of attacking the village if he thought it feasible. Terry and Gibbon continued on their way while Custer departed. Shortly after this Gibbon fell sick and he had to rest for a couple of days. Terry and the Montana column remained with him. Custer had meanwhile found what he took to be the hostile village and approached it from the east thus completing the pincer movement; Crook from the south, Terry and Gibbon from the north and Custer himself from the east. Unfortunately for him, Crook had not thought fit to tell anyone that he wasn't coming and Custer was unaware of Gibbon's delay. The 7th cavalry and their commander were about to take on the whole Sioux nation and their allies.

Striking the trail of the hostiles Custer soon ascertained their whereabouts. What he didn't know was their strength. Throughout the spring more and more Indians had left their reservations where they had spent the winter, and had gone to join the Sioux and Cheyenne at the Little Big Horn. By now there were thousands of them.

As he saw the village, or some of it, Custer divided his command as was usual when attacking Indians as they usually fled to nearby rocks and gullies from which they could snipe at the soldiers.

He sent Major Reno and his battalion to his left and Captain Benteen and his battalion to the left of Reno. He himself with his battalion occupied the position on the extreme right. All was set for the showdown.

Custer advanced along the line of bluffs while Reno and Benteen made their way down into the valley of the Little Big Horn; there they parted, Benteen went away to his left as ordered while Reno advanced upon the village crossing the Little Big Horn as he went.

All unsuspecting Charles and Sarah were dawdling out side their tipee when suddenly the alarm was sounded. Loud yells were heard;

"Long knives! Pony soldiers! They come!"

There was a sudden rush of Indians towards their horses while the non-combatants, squaws and children, fled, some on horse back but the majority of them on foot.

The Sioux and their allies rushed to form a firing line opposing Reno and his men. Rifle fire crackled along the line. Soldiers began to fall.

Charles, recovering from the surprise, seized Sarah by the arm.

"Git, while you can. This will be no place for a squaw. Look! All the squaws are leaving, join them. Hurry. If the soldiers get here they won't be too choosy about their targets."

Sarah refused. She didn't want to leave Charles.

"I'm not leaving you. Come with me if you like, but I'm not going without you."

"Don't be a fool Sarah. Go with the other squaws."

Sarah clung to him, her arms around his neck.

"I'm not going without you; you can't make me. Charley I love you. Please don't stay. Come away with me. Don't stay; you'll get hurt or killed, I know it. I couldn't bear it if anything should happen to you."

She loved him! This was a revelation to say the least. She picked a fine time to tell him. He was adamant however.

"You must go with the other squaws, Sarah. I will most likely have some fighting to do before this day is over. I'll fight better if I know you are safe. It's not too late. Look; there go some more squaws. Join them, please for my sake.

When this is all over you can come back if we are victorious; if not you will be well out of it."

Sarah began to sob; her tears trickled down her cheeks. She kissed him suddenly and then tore herself away and went after the squaws. Charley watched her go. She was almost identical to the other squaws with her long dark hair and her Sioux type dress and moccasins. She was the right height too to pass as a Sioux. She should be alright.

She glanced back once and then hurried on after the other squaws. Bullets began to whine around Charles' head, suddenly he saw 'Little White Bird', she was standing near her tipee watching the fighting. Charles called out to her. She was startled but responded after a moments hesitation.

"What are you doing, Princess?" Charles demanded. "You should go with the squaws and children. This will be no place for you."

She shook her head;

"I stay, Charlee. No go. I will see my vision come true. The pony-soldiers will be defeated. I stay."

Charles made an effort to appeal to her.

"Princess, I love you; this you must know already. When this is all over we can be married. Please go with the squaws."

It was no use, she stubbornly refused. She would stay to see her vision fulfilled come what may. She moved away then leaving Charles to contemplate the scene before him.

Reno was having a tough fight in the valley; he had lost a lot of men and was becoming panicky. All at once his nerve went and he ordered a retreat across the Little Big Horn and into the cover of the woodlands there. His men followed, splashing across the river and losing more soldiers as they did so. Even there they were not safe as the Indians infiltrated amongst the trees and picked them off easily. Reno was by now in a state of extreme panic; he now led a retreat back to the bluffs where he had parted from Custer. He left his men to follow as best they could. Down in the valley and across the Little Big Horn lay the bodies of more than sixty soldiers and several civilian scouts. He and the remainder of his battalion sought refuge on a hill known afterwards as Reno hill. There he was besieged by the Indians who circled him and sniped away from their cover amongst the rocks and trees surrounding the hill.

He had many wounded men who were unable to get medical aid and who lay there on the hill suffering extremes of thirst. Attempts to fetch water from a nearby stream by volunteers merely resulted in their being shot by the surrounding Indians.

There he remained until Captain Benteen arrived with his men. He had, it will be remembered, gone off to the left of Reno's force. He had circled around until he arrived back at his starting point on the bluffs. He had seen no Indians at all and wondered what all the shooting was about. Now he was back with Reno and his first question was 'where is Custer?'

Reno didn't know, and what's more, didn't care, all he was concerned about was getting himself and his men safely out of the Indians. He begged Benteen to stay and help him.

"I've been badly whipped," he told Benteen, "you've got to stay and help me."

Benteen agreed and so he joined Reno and left Custer to his fate. Before long he found himself besieged by the Sioux and unable to move away even if he wanted to.

Custer by this time had advanced along the crest of the bluffs and had reached a point from which he could gaze down into the valley and see, for the first time, the extent of the Indian village. He sent an urgent message to Benteen to tell him to come quickly to his aid. In the meantime he engaged the Indians as best he could. Soon it was apparent that he was getting the worst of it and he ordered a retreat to a hill behind; there they would have a better chance of standing off the Sioux and Cheyenne.

Alas, he never made it; Crazy Horse had taken part in the defeat of Reno and after that had led his warriors in a great sweeping movement around the base of the bluffs and onto Custer's flank. Now he attacked; sweeping over the crest of the hill and onto Custer. The fight didn't last long, a few minutes only, and all the soldiers including Custer were dead. The Sioux and their allies were triumphant; they prowled around the battlefield scalping the dead and administering the coup-de-gras to the wounded.

It was all over; Reno and Benteen stayed where they were until the following day when the Indians left before Terry and Gibbon arrived. Over 250 troopers were lying dead on the battlefield. A great victory for the Indians.

While this was going on Charles had been fighting his own battle against the Crow and Aricarree Indian scouts who accompanied the soldiers.

These scouts had crossed the Little Big Horn and reached the pony herd in the village. They intended to steal the ponies and possibly loot the now deserted tipees. Charles divined their intentions and determined to stop them. The pony herd was now depleted as most of them had been seized and mounted by the warriors at the first alarm, but there were enough of them left to satisfy the desires of the scouts.

As they approached the ponies Charles levelled his rifle and fired; it was meant as a warning shot. The effect upon the Aricarree scouts was unexpected, instead of turning back from their mission they returned his fire. Bullets whistled around him. He took cover as soon as he could. Their shooting was poor as usual but Charles took no risks, he kept under cover and tried another shot at them as soon as they ceased shooting.

They were perhaps surprised to see a white-eyes in the Sioux village but as Charles was wearing a Sioux hunting shirt, courtesy of Sarah, they assumed, rightly, that he was a Sioux at heart; anyway they commenced shooting once more. Charles was reluctant to kill any of them but he was left with little choice. He took careful aim and waited for one of them to show himself. He waited for several minutes it seemed before a head cautiously appeared from behind a tipee. He fired, and the Indian fell dead. That was the signal for the others to flee. They leaped on their ponies and galloped off back over the Little Big Horn. Charles came out of his cover and slowly approached the dead Indian. He put down his rifle and crouched down beside the fallen man to ascertain whether he was truly dead or merely wounded. It was a stupid thing to do and he realised it immediately. There was a sudden movement away to his left, without pausing for thought he drew his six-gun as swiftly as he could. It was hardly fast enough though and the Indian got his shot in first, fortunately he missed and the bullet sang past Charles' ear. He fired twice, his first shot missing by a considerable margin, but his second shot hit the target. The

Indian fell dead, shot through the heart. His companions across the river raised their voices in shouts of anger but were not keen to renew hostilities. Charles heaved a sigh of relief.

The shooting and yelling from the main battle had by now subsided and all was peaceful once more. The Sioux and their allies began to return triumphant in their victory. 'Little White Bird' was jubilant, she greeted Charles accordingly;

"Oh Charlee! This is great day for the Sioux. Now you believe in the Great Spirit, don't you? He predicted this and it has come to pass. We must celebrate."

That night the Sioux danced in celebration of their victory. Charles was happy for them, but he felt for the dead soldiers of whom he had once been one. He might have been lying out on the hillside with the others if fate had not decreed otherwise.

Next day the scouts brought the news that Generals Terry and Gibbon were at last approaching. The whole village packed up and departed, not having enough ammunition for another pitched battle. The Hunkpapas under Sitting Bull fled Northwards eventually reaching the Canadian border. The Ogallalas under Crazy Horse went to the South.

Charles had final words with his 'Princess'.

"Where will you go? Southwards? My folks have a ranch not very far away, you would be very welcome there."

She shook her head;

"I go with Crazy Horse. Maybe the Great Spirit has not finished with me. Come with us, Charlee."

Charles had to decline the invitation; he had Sarah to find. She had not returned with the other squaws.

"You go, Princess, I will stay behind and search for my squaw. I will catch up with you later. Princess, you know how I feel about you. If you feel the same about me then wait for me. I will find you if I'm still alive. Go now before it's too late."

So his 'Princess' departed with the Sioux who followed Crazy Horse. They followed a Southerly course for several days until they bumped into General Crook and his men. Then followed a fierce fight which ended with Crook being defeated once again by Crazy Horse. After that the Sioux were pursued relentlessly until, after another fight with the soldiers, they had to surrender. Crazy Horse had too many women and children with him; they sufferd greatly during the journey South, food was scarce and they had to keep almost continusly on the move. That was the end for the Sioux; they were put onto a reservation where life was pretty grim.

The remainder of the Sioux under Sitting Bull fled Northwards pursued by the army until they reached and crossed the border with Canada. There they settled and were safe for the time being.

All this was lost on Charles; he searched everywhere for Sarah. There were no clues as to her wereabouts; no-one he questioned had recalled seeing her and yet he knew that she had fled with the other squaws when the soldiers had attacked. Where was she?

She might have been killed; she looked very much like a Sioux squaw, the soldiers would be inclined to shoot without ascertaining her identity. She may have taken the chance to run away back to her own people, but Charles recalled her last words to him. She had declared her love for him and he couldn't belive that she would desert him like that. All this was passing through his mind, but the fact remained that she was missing. Where was she? He spent nine days searching for her without any luck. Then he gave up for the time being and set off after his 'Princess'.

He had no luck there either; there was no sign of the Ogallalla or any other Sioux tribe. They must have been rounded up and placed on the reservation. That was the conclusion to which Charles came. Accordingly he searched the Sioux reservations for many days and found nothing. There were plenty of Indians who remembered 'Little White Bird' but no-one knew what had happened to her.

After making a last search for Sarah he turned his horse for home. He was sad about his two females but didn't know what more he could do. He would get a warm welcome at home, he knew; his mother, father and his sister would welcome him enthusiastically.

Chapter 9   Abigail

CHARLES WAS RIGHT; his parents and sister made him welcome, his mother in particular was happy to have him back. She had been dreadfully afraid that he had been killed when she received the news of the Little Big Horn. Now there he was alive and unharmed. She wept tears of joy, poor woman. His father had always known that he would return unscathed, or so he claimed. His sister, Rachel was critical of his behaviour. She upbraided him for causing them all the worry, but she was very glad to have him back safe at last.

They listened sympathetically to his story of his women and tried to console him on his loss. Charles, after a day resting, turned his hand to assisting his father with the ranch. He worked steadily day after day doing the work of an ordinary cow-hand. His father already employed six cowboys and a foreman and as Charles didn't want to interfere with that arrangement, he just tagged along with them. He worked steadily and successfully for several days until one day as he was tidying up after corralling some horses, he espied a lone rider approaching from the direction of the town, Jackson Ford.

The rider was approaching fast and sat the horse confidently. As the rider came nearer Charles made out that it was a female.

She was dressed in a white blouse, long-sleeved, a short brown waist-coat, a long brown skirt and a cream-coloured Stetson. She was very good-looking and fairly young, about twenty-two. She rode her horse into the yard and stopped. There she stared at Charles for a minute or so.

"Well, dang my britches!" She exclaimed at last, "If it ain't Charley Cunningham for sure."

Charles grinned at her.

"Howdy Abigail; nice to see you again. Your language hasn't improved it seems. How you been keeping?"

The young girl didn't answer, she just sat her horse and waited patiently. After a minute or so she spoke.

"Well, are you going to take my horse or not?"

"Sure am, Abigail".

Charles took her horse by the bridle and led him to a hitching rail. There he tied him and waited. Abigail grew impatient.

"Help me down, Charlie please."

Charles complied. He knew perfectly well that she didn't need help in mounting or dismounting; she was a perfectly accomplished and competent horse rider. What's more Abigail knew that Charles was well aware of her ability; maybe she just wanted to feel his arms around her again.

She swung her leg over the horse's back and lowered herself into Charles' arms. He held her firmly, his hands grasping her well rounded hips. He held her like that for a few seconds until she demanded that he put her down. To do so he allowed her to slip down between his hands thus giving himself the chance to grasp her waist. It was so slim and firm!

"Darn it!" She exclaimed. "That's enough Charley! Don't you dare let your hands stray any further or I'll fetch you such a clout as will make your head sing. That's better". She alighted upon the ground slightly ruffled. She glared at Charles.

"You don't seem to have changed much; still free with your paws. I'm going now to pay my respects to your ma' and pa' and your sister. You wait here until I return, you and I have some talking to do."

With that she disappeared in the direction of the ranch-house. Charles returned to his work. After a long interval Abigail reappeared. She made straight for Charles. He regarded her with some interest, after all she was a real beauty with her light brown hair, long, but tucked up under her Stetson for the moment. Her eyes were a shade of hazel, her nose was finely chiselled and cute; her mouth was firm and her lips were well-shaped. When she smiled a row of perfectly white teeth was exposed. Her figure was perfect and her legs were well shaped. She wore a skirt that was split to allow her to straddle a horse and her feet and legs were encased in black, highly polished riding-boots. She was a tall girl, nearly as tall as Charles, and he was an inch or so short of six feet.

She approached him and halted when about two feet away. She looked at him sternly.

"Well, what have you to say for yourself?" She demanded.

"What d'ye mean, Abigail? What do you want me to say?"

Abigail nearly exploded.

"What do I mean? Why you ornery low down critter. You been away for two years with never a word of where you was and now you ask what do I want. Where you been Charlie? Why did you do it? We were all set I thought. My twenty-first birthday was nigh and I thought you might ask me to marry you. Instead you just up and away to live with the Indians. Resigned your commission in the army too. Why Charlie, why? You never breathed a word to me, just took yourself off and left me. I hoped you would come back soon and I cried myself to sleep for nigh on two months, hoping all the time that you would return, but you never did. I thought each day that to-morrow you would be back to claim me. Why did you do it? You rotten bastard."

"Why, Abigail, I just wanted a bit of space to sort things out in my mind. I didn't mean you no harm."

"Well I wasn't to know that. Anyway you got your space. Why didn't you come back? I waited for you Charlie. I thought you might send for me. I'd have come too. I would have been your squaw. You can smile, but it's true. I would have cooked for you, done your mending and washing and had your babies if you saw fit to give me any, and I would have nursed you when you was sick. Instead you just forgot about me. You had a squaw I suppose. What was she like; not as good-looking as me I dare say."

Charles waited until she ran out of breath then he explained;

"Sure, I had a squaw; not the kind you think though. She was white."

"She was what? White! Pull the other one Charlie. White indeed!"

Charles smiled at that;

"It's true. She was white. The Sioux captured her off a wagon-train and gave her to me. She was quite nice looking too."

"How old was she? Sixteen, twenty? Tell me Charlie."

"She was thirty-two or thirty-three," Charles replied.

"Thirty-three! Jumping Jiminy! She was old enough to be your grandmother. Did you have any young ones?"

"No we didn't, things weren't like that."

"Things weren't like that!" She scoffed.

"What were they like, Charlie? Tell me."

Charles tried to explain his relationship with Sarah. Whether he got through to Abigail or no he couldn't tell.

"So, Charlie, you and she lived happily ever after. Where is she now? Deserted her I shouldn't wonder."

"She went missing after the Greasy Grass fight."

"After the what?" Abigail asked.

"Sorry, I forgot; after the Little Big Horn. When the soldiers attacked all the squaws and children fled to safety. When it was all over they returned. Sarah didn't. I searched everywhere I could think, but I didn't find her."

Abigail grinned;

"So you lost your little squaw. You sure got a way with women, Charlie. Now if it had been me you wouldn't have got out of it so easy."

Charles didn't tell her about 'Little White Bird' she wouldn't have understood. Abigail thought for a few minutes and then;

"Well Charles, what are you going to do now?"

"I guess I'll just settle down on our ranch fer a spell. How about you? You ain't told me yet who you married after all."

Abigail's eyes blazed with fury; she took one step nearer to Charles and then slapped him firmly about the face.

"Ouch!" He cried, "Abigail that hurt."

"It was meant to, you ornery polecat. Who did I marry indeed! I ain't married to anybody. I waited fer you, and I want my head looking at I can tell. You lousy good fer nothing'."

Charles was stunned; not married! He was sure that an attractive girl like Abigail would be married by now.

"Why Abigail," he exclaimed, "not married! You must have had some offers fer sure."

"I had plenty of offers, well, three or four, but I turned them all down. I wanted you Charlie. I waited fer you. Now I'm twenty-two and in a fair way to being an old maid, and all because of you."

Charles shook his head; here was a fine state of things. There was Sarah, if she were still alive, looking for him possibly, and 'Little White Bird' somewhere too. He didn't see fit to tell Abigail about her; it wouldn't do any good and would probably just complicate matters further.

"Well, Abigail," he said, "what do you want me to do now?"

"What do I want you to do? Why you no good so-and-so, I want you to make up yore mind. Are we to resume our relationship or no? Charlie, you will have to make up yore mind."

"Sure, I'll make up my mind. I'll like it fine if we could carry on where we left off."

Abigail was pleased with his decision.

"Charlie, I'm putting you on three weeks trial. You better behave yourself in that time. If you don't or if you haven't made up yore mind to marry me, it's all off and I'll marry Harry Wells."

"Who in hell is Harry Wells? Where'd he come from? He's a new one on me."

"He's a major in the cavalry, and he's sweet on me. You better watch yoreself Charlie".

Charles smiled;

"The life of an army wife ain't a bed of roses," he said, "you would find it pretty hard going, stuck on some remote army post miles away from anywhere."

Abigail was not impressed by this information.

"Well, Charlie, if you are serious you can take me to the Friday night dance. Call for me around seven o'clock. Don't be late."

"The Friday dance! They still have them! All the cowhands, hayseeds and good for nothings go, or they used to."

Abigail sniffed, she made for her horse.

"Help me mount Charlie, please."

Once again Charles knew that she could very well mount without any help from him, nevertheless he assisted her. She arrived in the saddle in a slightly ruffled state.

"Gold darn it Charlie, if you don't keep your hands where they belong I'll fetch you another clout to go with the other one."

"I thought you'd like it, Abigail. Just like old times."

"It's nothing like old times. See you on Friday at seven; don't ferget."

Charles watched her ride away; what a girl! He could do worse he thought. He watched her until she disappeared into the distance, then he turned his attention to his work once more.

Friday night came at last and Charles presented himself at the Anson house at seven o'clock precisely. Mr. and Mrs. Anson were pleased to see him again and made him most welcome. Abigail was not quite ready, as expected; Charles waited

impatiently for her, not like a Sioux squaw he thought. At length she descended from her bed-room and greeted Charles enthusiastically. She was looking as lovely as ever in her full-length dress of blue and white.

"You sure look great," Charles declared, "just as I remember you."

"Well, I thought I ought to make an effort, after all Charlie you been used to those Sioux squaws and all. Let's go, then. You got a buckboard or something ?"

"Why, Abigail, there's no buckboard. I reckoned we could walk. It ain't far."

"Damn it all Charlie, I wasn't aiming to walk in this dress. If I get it dirty, or if it rains while we're awalking you'll be needing the services or a good surgeon."

Charles merely smiled and offered his arm. They walked slowly on towards the dance-hall. It was a fine night with never a hint of rain. Abigail made a fine partner for any man. The dance was successful and enjoyed by both. The walk back afterwards was made more enjoyable for Charles as Abigail took his arm and snuggled up to him. Dare he kiss her? A year or so ago he wouldn't have hesitated, and she would have expected it of him, but now after all that time, he wasn't sure.

He decided to risk it.

"Darn it, Charlie, you're full of surprises. Just remember, you ain't got any privileges any more. That is, until I tell you otherwise. Now just get me home safe and I'll be quite happy."

He got her home alright, wished her a good night, thanked her for the evening, and departed. He got his horse from the livery stable and made his way home. It had been a most enjoyable night, pity she wouldn't let him kiss her again, but then one couldn't have everything.

Chapter 10 The Ultimatum.

A FEW DAYS later Charles was in the town of Jackson Ford to collect supplies for the ranch; while he was there he decided to call on Abigail and see how she was getting along.

Abigail was pleased to see him and made him most welcome. He had a pleasant time with her and her folks until he bethought himself of the business which had brought him to the town in the first place. He took his leave with some reluctance. Abigail promised to call on him later in the week and so he had to be content with that.

He called at the various stores and purchased his supplies which he carried to the wagon which he had brought. He was all ready to climb aboard and move off when suddenly he heard his name called.

"Hi there! Charlie Cunningham. What yuh doin' here? The Indians kick yuh out? Yuh shore don't have much luck do yuh? First the army and now the Indians. Ah heard they was mighty mad at yuh for messing with their squaws. Now yuh come back home to mess with our women."

Charlie identified his tormentor.

"Well, well, if it ain't Bully Biggins. How you doing Bully? They still let you live here? Make the most of it Bully, it can't last, then you'll be heaved out."

"My name is William as yuh well know," responded the other, "Billy to my friends of which yuh ain't one."

Charles grinned;

"Yuh was always known as Bully in the good old days. I don't see no need to change now. See yuh later, Bully, so long."

He made to climb onto his wagon when 'Bully' Biggins caught hold of his sleeve.

"Not so fast, Cunningham. I promised to punch yuh on the nose next time I saw yuh for what yuh did to Abigail. Now's a good a time as any."

Charles halted his attempt to climb aboard the wagon.

"Just you try it, Bully. See where it gets yuh. What's it to you what passed between Abigail and myself?"

"Abigail's a nice girl and she don't need you and your Indian ways. I'm going to give yuh a whopping you won't fergit in a hurry."

"Suit yoreself, Bully, but I ain't packing a gun."

"That's alright," 'Bully' replied, "I ain't packing one neither."

The two young men moved a few yards to obtain a clear field of action and then they went at it hammer and tongs.

They were fairly evenly matched, 'Bully' being an inch or so taller and a few pounds heavier. Charles was the fitter of the two however.

After grappling each other a few times they fell to throwing punches. It soon became obvious who threw the heavier punch. Charles began to take some punishment. At last a punch from his opponent floored him. He lay on the ground dazed somewhat.

"How d'ye like that, Indian lover?" 'Bully' cried triumphantly.

Charles shook his head to clear it and struggled to his feet.

"This here fight's not over yet," he declared.

They started again, this time Charles was a little more cautious. At last he got in a decisive punch and it was his opponents turn to hit the dirt.

"How's that take yuh, 'Bully' he cried.

'Bully' Biggins was not too taken with it, nevertheless he struggled to his feet and, giving vent to some blood -thirsty threats, he resumed the fight.

It wasn't long before he had Charles down once more. This time it was a full-bloodied blow to the jaw.

Charles took his time in regaining his feet and he stood there swaying precariously while his opponent recommenced punching him. Suddenly Charles seized hold of 'Bully' and threw him to the ground. There they sprawled locked together while they punched and clawed each other.

A large crowd had gathered to watch consisting of males and a few females all cheering first one contestant then the other. It was difficult to say who was getting the best of it, each landed a few punches on his opponent and Charles managed to bang 'Bullys' head against the ground a few times which did nothing to improve his temper. On the other hand 'Bully' landed one or two telling blows on Charles' face and body. It was difficult to say who would come off best when there came an unexpected interruption.

The marshal and his deputy arrived; he drew his gun and ordered the fight to stop at once.

"He started it, Marshal," Charles exclaimed.

"I don't give a damn who started it. I'm stopping it right now. If yuh don't stop I'll bend this gun-barrel over your heads."

They stopped and scrambled to their feet. They were dusty and dishevelled, bleeding and bruised. The marshal and the deputy seized hold of them and marched them off to the courthouse. There the judge just happened to be sitting · waiting for them. They were charged with being disorderly and violent on the streets of the town.

"Disorderly and disgraceful conduct", the judge said, "fined five dollars and costs."

"Costs! What costs?" Charles asked.

"The costs to cover the marshal's and his deputy's time dealing with you two ruffians," the judge explained rather severely.

Billy Biggins paid up straight away, but Charles had no money on his person having spent it all on the supplies for the ranch.

"Well, in that case," the judge said, "you'll have to be locked up until the fine is paid. Take him away, marshal."

Charles, protesting vigorously, was led away to the jail which was situated as an annex to the marshal's office. There he stayed until his fine was paid. This didn't happen for two days when his sister at last appeared with the money. There was a charge for the food and accommodation too. Charles was worried that Rachel wouldn't have enough money but he needn't have concerned himself; she had brought sufficient for all eventualities.

Charles was pleased to see her as might have been expected. She had brought the buckboard for them and Charles took the reins and started to drive them both home. As they passed down the street there was a loud guffaw.

"Charlie Cunningham taken home by a girl! Haw, haw! Get her to put some ointment on them bruises on yore face, Charlie. Any time yuh feel like collecting some more just come into town and look me up. Haw! Haw!"

It was, of course, Billy Biggins. Charles glared at him as they passed.

"Take no heed, Charlie," Rachel said, "just ignore him."

An hour later they were back at the ranch where Charles was welcomed warmly by his mother and father.

A few days after Abigail turned up at the ranch. She was smartly dressed as usual as she rode up to the barn where Charles was working.

"Well howdy, Abigail, nice to see yuh again."

She didn't reply; instead she dismounted without assistance and walked her horse to a hitching rail where she tied him. Only then did she speak.

"Howdy, Charles. My your face does look a mess. Billy Biggins sure knocked yuh around and no mistake. He said he would next time he saw yuh."

Charles was annoyed.

"He didn't knock me about; yuh should see his face."

"I have; there's hardly a mark on it. What were you fighting about anyway?"

"We were fighting over yuh. Biggins said I treated yuh badly."

"Well, well," said Abigail, "I must treat Billy with a little more consideration in future. Maybe I'll let him take me to the dance."

Charles was appalled by the thought.

"Surely, Abigail, yuh ain't going soft on Billy; he ain't your type."

"Don't get yourself in a sweat; I said I might let him take me to the dance. Anyhow, that's not what I came about. I been thinking hard about yuh and me. I'm telling yuh, Charlie, yuh have three weeks to make up yore mind about me. Three weeks, Charlie, that's all, then I'm taking up with Major Harry Wells if he'll have me."

If he would have her! He would jump at the chance as Charlie well knew, so did Abigail if it came to that. Oh, she knew what she was doing alright.

"I don't need three weeks, Abigail, I've made up my mind already."

"I wish I could be sure of that, Charlie. I've waited a year and a half for yuh, and I ain't waiting much longer. Yuh think about it real hard for three weeks, then let me know. I thought yuh and me was all ready to tie the knot once afore but yuh up and ran off to the Indians. Yuh left me, Charlie, yuh swine, but I'll forgive yuh and give yuh another chance. Three weeks; that's all I'm giving yuh. Don't ferget."

After that she visited Charlie's folks and his sister before returning to her horse. She mounted, waved goodbye to Charles, and galloped off.

He was left to gaze after her in admiration. He had three weeks to think carefully about the situation. Three weeks! Why, he wouldn't need three weeks, nor even three minutes. His mind was made up; or was it?

He thought then about Sarah. Where was she? What had happened to her? The thought that she might be lying out on the prairie somewhere dead filled him with horror. Surely she couldn't be. The more he thought about it the more he became distressed; his blood ran cold.

Then he thought about 'Little White Bird' his Princess; where was she? What had happened to her? She might be anywhere, still having the dreams and visions. The Great Spirit might have finished with her, in which case she would be free to marry. Her father might force her to marry a Sioux! Again his blood turned to water. His Princess a squaw of some Sioux brave. Poor little girl, she wouldn't know if Charles were alive or not. She wouldn't know if he were married to someone else or no.

He must find out what had happened to each of them before the three weeks were up.

Abigail was a very nice and caring girl, but was she the right one for him?

Chapter 11 The Search.

RACHEL WAS QUITE hard on her brother. She did not approve of the way he treated Abigail and Sarah. No matter that Sarah had gone with the squaws, he should have made sure that she was safe and knew where to find him. It was in vain that Charles tried to explain that he didn't know where to search for her. No-one had recalled seeing her, and he had expected her to return almost at once.

"You must have treated her very badly, Charles," Rachel said, "poor girl, she didn't want to return to you."

Charles was about to remind her of Sarah's last words to him, but he thought better of it. He was in something of a dilemma; if he married Abigail and Sarah turned up later it might prove awkward to say the least. True, Sarah and he had not been formally married, but they had lived together and that might not go down too well with Abigail if she were reminded of it.

Sarah might make trouble for him, at the very least she might prove difficult to appease. Abigail, he was sure, would stick by him but things would be difficult and their relationship might be a trifle strained.

On the other hand he could hardly ask Abigail to wait until he searched once again for Sarah. Supposing he found her? What then?

The situation with 'Little White Bird' was hardly less complicated. Where was she? What had happened to her? Was she dead? If she were still alive had the Great Spirit finished with her? Was she still receiving dreams and visions? If so she would not marry. He would have to wait, perhaps for ever. If, on the other hand, her dreams and visions had ceased and she was free to marry, her father might force her to marry a Sioux brave. He recalled how they had promised to marry once she was free, but she may not know where he was and if he had kept his side of the arrangement.

There again, he couldn't ask Abigail to wait until he found his Princess and ascertained her status. 'Abigail my dear, wait until I find my Princess; if she's free to marry then I'll marry her, if not then I'll marry you.'

No, no, that wouldn't do. He could imagine the kind of reply Abigail would give him. It wasn't as if he was asking for a few days grace; no, it probably would take considerably longer than the three weeks she had given him.

In his dilemma he consulted his sister. She was not very sympathetic.

"It's your own fault, Charles," she said, "you should have shown more consideration for Abigail. Now you stand to lose her and the others. What have you been doing? Enjoying yourself by the sound of it. Well, now you have to face the consequences. Abigail, or one of the others, it's your choice."

"Thank you very much, Rachel, for that sage advice. It helps a lot, I don't think."

Charles continued in a state of indecision for several more days then he made up his mind. He would go for one last search and then if he didn't find either of his women he would marry Abigail.

Charles took a few days off from his father's ranch and searched everywhere he could think of. He found nothing; at least nothing of any interest to him. He came back to the ranch with his mind made up at last; Abigail it would be.

He waited though until the three weeks were up, it would never do to let her know that he was anxious to marry her. A few more days wouldn't hurt.

He was out on the prairie one day soon after his return when one of the cow-boys out there with him called him over.

"Say, boss, there's a party of Indians over yonder by the river. Cheyenne, I think. They seem to want something but they don't savvy our language."

Charles was interested; it would be a pleasant change to speak to them. The Cheyenne language wasn't so very different from the Sioux. He mounted his horse and went to the riverside. There he found a bunch of Miniconjou Sioux, about eight of them.

He greeted them in their own language which came as a surprise to them. They showed their relief at finding a white-eyes with whom they could converse.

It transpired that they were starving; the food on the reservation was not enough for them all, their women and children were suffering. They wondered if they could have a steer or two to help out their meagre rations. They were forbidden to hunt the buffalo, they told Charles.

Charles thought for a minute, then he gave orders for his men to cut out a couple of steers from the herd. This being done, and the animals checked to make sure they were in good condition, he let the Indians take them. This they did with gratitude.

Later, when he got home, he told his father what he had done.

"That's alright, son," his father said, "but we can't give away too many of our cattle. There won't be enough to sell if you do that too often."

Anyhow, the Miniconjou were happy with their steers. Charles asked them about

'Little White Bird' but they had nothing to tell, in fact, they had never heard of her.

Charles continued to work on the ranch and time passed; the three weeks were up and Abigail would be waiting. He decided to let her wait a few days more; his mind was made up though.

When he considered that he had kept her waiting long enough he called upon her. That she would throw herself into his arms he didn't doubt for a minute. It was Mrs. Anson who answered the door. She gasped when she saw Charles standing there. She seemed flustered. Charles greeted her with a smile.

"Howdy, Mrs. Anson. I've called to see Abigail. Is she around?"

Mrs. Anson just stared at him in bewilderment. Abigail's voice called from upstairs just then.

"Who is it, Ma'?"

Her mother answered in a trembley voice,

"It's Charlie Cunningham. He wants to see you."

Abigail gave vent to a most unlady-like expression which was easily audible to her visitor. A moment later and she was descending the stairs rapidly. She arrived at the bottom breathless and in a state of slight undress. She pitched into Charles right away.

"Charlie Cunningham! How dare you call upon me now. Your time-limit was up five days ago as you must well know. I waited an extra day for yuh but yuh didn't show. Major Wells proposed to me two days ago and I accepted him. We are to be married in four weeks. Yuh had your chance, Charlie, and yuh blew it."

"Abigail! Yuh can't mean it! I thought we was meant for each other. Damn Major Wells. Well yuh can just break it off with him. I want yuh."

Abigail stamped her foot.

"Git lost, Charlie. I've had enough of yuh. Keeping me awaiting and awaiting while yuh make up your mind. Charles Cunningham, goodbye. If ever we meet again I'll acknowledge yuh, but that's all. Now git!"

Charles departed in some despair. Abigail to be married! Not to him either. He couldn't believe it.

He was fairly quiet over the next few days, his parents and sister wondered what the trouble was but didn't like to ask. Rachel had a pretty shrewd idea.

"It's Abigail," she said, "something's gone wrong. I wouldn't be surprised if she had turned him down. He was going to propose to her if you recall. Serve him right if she has."

Eventually he confided in Rachel. She expressed no surprise at all. Nor was she in the least bit sympathetic.

"If you treated me like that, Charlie, I'd have boxed your ears right smartly and sent you packing."

That was more or less what Abigail had done. Perhaps Charlie had spent too long with the Sioux. He had forgotten, if he ever knew, how to treat a white girl, especially one who loved him, Rachel reflected.

"Well. Charlie, you'll just have to get over it and get on with your work. You've been slacking recently. Father has made allowances for you so far, but he won't much longer."

After a few days Charles threw himself into his work and tried to forget about Abigail. This helped him until one day he heard about Abigail's wedding. He had obviously not been invited. Just as well, he thought, Major Wells might have got himself a bloody nose. Charles made an effort and got over his disappointment.

A month later he met the party of Miniconjou Sioux; they greeted each other affably. They wondered if they might have another steer or two. Charles saw to it that their request was granted. There was no news of his Princess. The Miniconjou went on their way driving the steers before them; Charles went on his way despairing.

Rachel was worried about her brother and tried to get him interested in other girls. This worked for a time, but eventually he gave over bothering about them. Rachel continued to be concerned.

"Charles, my dear," she said, "you'll have to accept the fact that your 'Little White Bird' and Sarah are gone. They are not coming back. Do try to become interested in some other girl. There are lots of very nice girls around. If you'd only try you could get yourself a very nice wife, if that's what you want."

Charles acknowledged Rachel's interest and her advice. She was right of course. He really must make an effort.

Weeks went by when suddenly he encountered an elderly squaw from the Ogallala Sioux. He was out on the prairie looking for strays when he came across the squaw. She was fairly ancient and on her last legs. He dismounted and went to her. She recognised him immediately.

"Ah, white-eyes," she said in a croakey voice, "it is good that I see you before I die.

I remember you were friends with the Sioux. Many moons have passed since those days. Are you the same? Are you a friend to the Sioux?"

Charles reassured her; he was still a friend of the Sioux. She nodded weakly.

"All my men folk are dead; killed by the white-eyes. Only I am left. When I pass to the Great Spirit bury me here on the prairie. Promise that, white-eyes."

Charles promised and sat with her holding her hand while she fell into a deep sleep.

An hour or two passed, still Charles held her hand. She opened her eyes suddenly.

"White-eyes," she croaked, "I go now. Bury me as I wish. 'Little White Bird' was right. You are the friend of the Indian."

Charles was startled to hear this. He squeezed her hand gently but firmly.

"Tell me, where is 'Little White Bird'? I have sought her for many moons. Where is she?"

The old woman smiled feebly.

"The white-eyes is a fool. Look near Bear mountain."

She closed her eyes.

"I go now white-eyes. Look to Bear mountain."

Her eyes remained closed now and her breathing became more laboured. It was not possible for Charles to say just when she died, it was a peaceful ending. He buried her as she requested. Then he set out for Bear mountain. His hopes were high. Bear mountain! Of course, why had he not thought of that before.

Bear mountain was not too far away and soon it came in sight. Charles' pulse beat faster and he began to become anxious. A few tepees came in sight now, about a dozen of them. When he got up to them he dismounted and looked about. A few Sioux were lounging around idly regarding the newcomer. A few squaws were busy with their chores but there was no sign of his Princess.

As he walked between the tepees he suddenly saw one at some distance from the others. It was a shade lighter than usual, almost white in fact. A few mystic symbols adorned it's exterior. Charles made his way over to it. All was quiet. He pushed aside the flap and peered in. The fire was gently smoking away as was the custom, and two beds were made up. A few blankets and trinkets were lying around but there was no one there. He let the flap drop and straightened up.

"The white-eyes seeks someone?"

The voice sounded clear in his ears. To him it was like music. He turned and beheld;

"Little White Bird! My lovely Princess. I have sought you many moons. Now I have found you at last."

'Little White Bird' smiled, a wonderful radiant smile; then he knew everything was alright.

"Princess, are you free? Do you still receive dreams and visions from the Great Spirit? Are you free to become my squaw?"

"Yes, Charlee. I am free. The Great Spirit has spoken. I am yours if you will have me. He still sends me visions and dreams but I am free to marry the white eyes, if he will have me."

Charles picked her up; what a nice little bundle she made!

"Come, Princess. I will take you to your new home. My mother, father and sister will make you very welcome. They will be very pleased that I found you at last. You will soon learn the white-eyes tongue, or they will learn Sioux."

Charles carried her to his horse; she lay comfortably in his arms. He kissed her.

"You took long time to find me, Charlee. The Great Spirit showed me in a vision that you sought me. You were very foolish; you should have come to Bear mountain sooner."

Charles mounted his horse with 'Little White Bird' mounted behind him. They rode slowly back to Charles' ranch where his folks awaited them.

THE END